THE GHOST-SHIP
AND OTHER STORIES

THE GHOST SHIP
& OTHER STORIES
By RICHARD MIDDLETON

WILDSIDE PRESS

Published by
Wildside Press, LLC
P.O. Box 301
Holicong, PA 18928-0301 USA
www.wildsidepress.com

Wildside Press Edition: MMIII

Thanks are due to the Editors of *The Century, The English Review, Vanity Fair,* and *The Academy,* for permission to reproduce most of the stories in this volume.

CONTENTS

CONTENTS

THE GHOST-SHIP

FAIRFIELD is a little village lying near the Portsmouth Road about half-way between London and the sea. Strangers who find it by accident now and then, call it a pretty, old-fashioned place; we who live in it and call it home don't find anything very pretty about it, but we should be sorry to live anywhere else. Our minds have taken the shape of the inn and the church and the green, I suppose. At all events we never feel comfortable out of Fairfield.

Of course the Cockneys, with their vasty houses and noise-ridden streets, can call us rustics if they choose, but for all that Fairfield is a better place to live in than London. Doctor says that when he goes to London his mind is bruised with the weight of the houses, and he was a Cockney born. He had to live there himself when he was a

little chap, but he knows better now. You
gentlemen may laugh—perhaps some of you
come from London way—but it seems to
me that a witness like that is worth a gallon
of arguments.

Dull? Well, you might find it dull, but
I assure you that I've listened to all the
London yarns you have spun to-night, and
they're absolutely nothing to the things that
happen at Fairfield. It's because of our way
of thinking and minding our own business.
If one of your Londoners were set down on
the green of a Saturday night when the
ghosts of the lads who died in the war keep
tryst with the lasses who lie in the churchyard, he couldn't help being curious and
interfering, and then the ghosts would go
somewhere where it was quieter. But we
just let them come and go and don't make
any fuss, and in consequence Fairfield is the
ghostiest place in all England. Why, I've
seen a headless man sitting on the edge of the
well in broad daylight, and the children playing about his feet as if he were their father.
Take my word for it, spirits know when
they are well off as much as human beings.

Still, I must admit that the thing I'm
going to tell you about was queer even for
our part of the world, where three packs of
ghost-hounds hunt regularly during the
season, and blacksmith's great-grandfather is
busy all night shoeing the dead gentlemen's
horses. Now that's a thing that wouldn't
happen in London, because of their interfering ways, but blacksmith he lies up aloft
and sleeps as quiet as a lamb. Once when
he had a bad head he shouted down to
them not to make so much noise, and in
the morning he found an old guinea left on
the anvil as an apology. He wears it on his
watch-chain now. But I must get on with
my story; if I start telling you about the
queer happenings at Fairfield I'll never stop.
It all came of the great storm in the
spring of '97, the year that we had two
great storms. This was the first one, and I
remember it very well, because I found in
the morning that it had lifted the thatch of
my pigsty into the widow's garden as
clean as a boy's kite. When I looked over
the hedge, widow—Tom Lamport's widow
that was—was prodding for her nasturtiums

with a daisy-grubber. After I had watched
her for a little I went down to the "Fox
and Grapes" to tell landlord what she had
said to me. Landlord he laughed, being a
married man and at ease with the sex.
"Come to that," he said, "the tempest has
blowed something into my field. A kind of
a ship I think it would be."

I was surprised at that until he explained
that it was only a ghost-ship and would do
no hurt to the turnips. We argued that
it had been blown up from the sea at
Portsmouth, and then we talked of something else. There were two slates down at
the parsonage and a big tree in Lumley's
meadow. It was a rare storm.

I reckon the wind had blown our ghosts
all over England. They were coming back
for days afterwards with foundered horses
and as footsore as possible, and they were
so glad to get back to Fairfield that some
of them walked up the street crying like
little children. Squire said that his great-
grandfather's great-grandfather hadn't looked
so dead-beat since the battle of Naseby, and
he's an educated man.

What with one thing and another, I should think it was a week before we got straight again, and then one afternoon I met the landlord on the green and he had a worried face. " I wish you'd come and have a look at that ship in my field," he said to me ; " it seems to me it's leaning real hard on the turnips. I can't bear thinking what the missus will say when she sees it."

I walked down the lane with him, and sure enough there was a ship in the middle of his field, but such a ship as no man had seen on the water for three hundred years, let alone in the middle of a turnip-field. It was all painted black and covered with carvings, and there was a great bay window in the stern for all the world like the Squire's drawing-room. There was a crowd of little black cannon on deck and looking out of her port-holes, and she was anchored at each end to the hard ground. I have seen the wonders of the world on picture-postcards, but I have never seen anything to equal that.

"She seems very solid for a ghost-ship," I said, seeing the landlord was bothered.

"I should say it's a betwixt and between,"

he answered, puzzling it over, "but it's going
to spoil a matter of fifty turnips, and missus
she'll want it moved." We went up to her
and touched the side, and it was as hard as
a real ship. "Now there's folks in England
would call that very curious," he said.

Now I don't know much about ships, but
I should think that that ghost-ship weighed
a solid two hundred tons, and it seemed to
me that she had come to stay, so that I felt
sorry for landlord, who was a married man.
"All the horses in Fairfield won't move her
out of my turnips," he said, frowning at
her.

Just then we heard a noise on her deck, and
we looked up and saw that a man had come
out of her front cabin and was looking down
at us very peaceably. He was dressed in a
black uniform set out with rusty gold lace,
and he had a great cutlass by his side in a
brass sheath. "I'm Captain Bartholomew
Roberts," he said, in a gentleman's voice, "put
in for recruits. I seem to have brought her
rather far up the harbour."

"Harbour!" cried landlord; "why, you're
fifty miles from the sea."

Captain Roberts didn't turn a hair. " So much as that, is it ? " he said coolly. " Well, it's of no consequence."

Landlord was a bit upset at this. " I don't want to be unneighbourly," he said, " but I wish you hadn't brought your ship into my field. You see, my wife sets great store on these turnips."

The captain took a pinch of snuff out of a fine gold box that he pulled out of his pocket, and dusted his fingers with a silk handkerchief in a very genteel fashion. " I'm only here for a few months," he said ; " but if a testimony of my esteem would pacify your good lady I should be content," and with the words he loosed a great gold brooch from the neck of his coat and tossed it down to landlord.

Landlord blushed as red as a strawberry. " I'm not denying she's fond of jewellery," he said, " but it's too much for half a sackful of turnips." And indeed it was a handsome brooch.

The captain laughed. " Tut, man," he said, " it's a forced sale, and you deserve a good price. Say no more about it ; " and nodding

good-day to us, he turned on his heel and
went into the cabin. Landlord walked back
up the lane like a man with a weight off his
mind. "That tempest has blowed me a bit
of luck," he said; "the missus will be main
pleased with that brooch. It's better than
blacksmith's guinea, any day."

Ninety-seven was Jubilee year, the year of
the second Jubilee, you remember, and we
had great doings at Fairfield, so that we hadn't
much time to bother about the ghost-ship,
though anyhow it isn't our way to meddle
in things that don't concern us. Landlord, he
saw his tenant once or twice when he was
hoeing his turnips and passed the time of day,
and landlord's wife wore her new brooch to
church every Sunday. But we didn't mix
much with the ghosts at any time, all except
an idiot lad there was in the village, and he
didn't know the difference between a man
and a ghost, poor innocent! On Jubilee Day,
however, somebody told Captain Roberts why
the church bells were ringing, and he hoisted
a flag and fired off his guns like a loyal
Englishman. 'Tis true the guns were shotted,
and one of the round shot knocked a hole in

Farmer Johnstone's barn, but nobody thought much of that in such a season of rejoicing.

It wasn't till our celebrations were over that we noticed that anything was wrong in Fairfield. 'Twas shoemaker who told me first about it one morning at the " Fox and Grapes." "You know my great great-uncle ? " he said to me.

" You mean Joshua, the quiet lad," I answered, knowing him well.

" Quiet ! " said shoemaker indignantly. " Quiet you call him, coming home at three o'clock every morning as drunk as a magistrate and waking up the whole house with his noise."

" Why, it can't be Joshua ! " I said, for I knew him for one of the most respectable young ghosts in the village.

" Joshua it is," said shoemaker ; " and one of these nights he'll find himself out in the street if he isn't careful."

This kind of talk shocked me, I can tell you, for I don't like to hear a man abusing his own family, and I could hardly believe that a steady youngster like Joshua had taken to drink. But just then in came butcher

Aylwin in such a temper that he could hardly
drink his beer. "The young puppy! the
young puppy!" he kept on saying; and it
was some time before shoemaker and I found
out that he was talking about his ancestor
that fell at Senlac.

"Drink?" said shoemaker hopefully, for
we all like company in our misfortunes, and
butcher nodded grimly.

"The young noodle," he said, emptying his
tankard.

Well, after that I kept my ears open, and
it was the same story all over the village.
There was hardly a young man among all the
ghosts of Fairfield who didn't roll home in
the small hours of the morning the worse for
liquor. I used to wake up in the night and
hear them stumble past my house, singing
outrageous songs. The worst of it was that
we couldn't keep the scandal to ourselves,
and the folk at Greenhill began to talk of
"sodden Fairfield" and taught their children
to sing a song about us:

"Sodden Fairfield, sodden Fairfield, has no use for
      bread-and-butter,
   Rum for breakfast, rum for dinner, rum for tea, and
      rum for supper!"

We are easy-going in our village, but we didn't like that.

Of course we soon found out where the young fellows went to get the drink, and landlord was terribly cut up that his tenant should have turned out so badly, but his wife wouldn't hear of parting with the brooch, so that he couldn't give the Captain notice to quit. But as time went on, things grew from bad to worse, and at all hours of the day you would see those young reprobates sleeping it off on the village green. Nearly every afternoon a ghost-wagon used to jolt down to the ship with a lading of rum, and though the older ghosts seemed inclined to give the Captain's hospitality the go-by, the youngsters were neither to hold nor to bind.

So one afternoon when I was taking my nap I heard a knock at the door, and there was parson looking very serious, like a man with a job before him that he didn't altogether relish. " I'm going down to talk to the Captain about all this drunkenness in the village, and I want you to come with me," he said straight out.

I can't say that I fancied the visit much

myself, and I tried to hint to parson that as, after all, they were only a lot of ghosts, it didn't very much matter.

"Dead or alive, I'm responsible for their good conduct," he said, "and I'm going to do my duty and put a stop to this continued disorder. And you are coming with me, John Simmons." So I went, parson being a persuasive kind of man.

We went down to the ship, and as we approached her I could see the Captain tasting the air on deck. When he saw parson he took off his hat very politely, and I can tell you that I was relieved to find that he had a proper respect for the cloth. Parson acknowledged his salute and spoke out stoutly enough. "Sir, I should be glad to have a word with you."

"Come on board, sir; come on board," said the Captain, and I could tell by his voice that he knew why we were there. Parson and I climbed up an uneasy kind of ladder, and the Captain took us into the great cabin at the back of the ship, where the bay-window was. It was the most wonderful place you ever saw in your life, all full of gold and silver plate, swords with jewelled scabbards, carved oak chairs, and great chests that look as though they were bursting with guineas. Even parson was surprised, and he did not shake his head very hard when the Captain took down some silver cups and poured us out a drink of rum. I tasted mine, and I don't mind saying that it changed my view of things entirely. There was nothing betwixt and between about that rum, and I felt that it was ridiculous to blame the lads for drinking too much of stuff like that. It seemed to fill my veins with honey and fire.

Parson put the case squarely to the Captain, but I didn't listen much to what he said ; I was busy sipping my drink and looking through the window at the fishes swimming to and fro over landlord's turnips. Just then it seemed the most natural thing in the world that they should be there, though afterwards, of course, I could see that that proved it was a ghost-ship.

But even then I thought it was queer when I saw a drowned sailor float by in the thin air with his hair and beard all full of bubbles.

It was the first time I had seen anything quite like that at Fairfield.

All the time I was regarding the wonders of the deep parson was telling Captain Roberts how there was no peace or rest in the village owing to the curse of drunkenness, and what a bad example the youngsters were setting to the older ghosts. The Captain listened very attentively, and only put in a word now and then about boys being boys and young men sowing their wild oats. But when parson had finished his speech he filled up our silver cups and said to parson, with a flourish, " I should be sorry to cause trouble anywhere where I have been made welcome, and you will be glad to hear that I put to sea to-morrow night. And now you must drink me a prosperous voyage." So we all stood up and drank the toast with honour, and that noble rum was like hot oil in my veins.

After that Captain showed us some of the curiosities he had brought back from foreign parts, and we were greatly amazed, though afterwards I couldn't clearly remember what they were. And then I found myself walking across the turnips with parson, and I was

telling him of the glories of the deep that
I had seen through the window of the ship.
He turned on me severely. "If I were you,
John Simmons," he said, "I should go straight
home to bed." He has a way of putting
things that wouldn't occur to an ordinary
man, has parson, and I did as he told me.

Well, next day it came on to blow, and it
blew harder and harder, till about eight o'clock
at night I heard a noise and looked out into
the garden. I dare say you won't believe me,
it seems a bit tall even to me, but the wind
had lifted the thatch of my pigsty into the
widow's garden a second time. I thought I
wouldn't wait to hear what widow had to say
about it, so I went across the green to the
"Fox and Grapes," and the wind was so
strong that I danced along on tip-toe like a
girl at the fair. When I got to the inn landlord had to help me shut the door; it seemed
as though a dozen goats were pushing against
it to come in out of the storm.

"It's a powerful tempest," he said, drawing
the beer. "I hear there's a chimney down at
Dickory End."

"It's a funny thing how these sailors know

about the weather," I answered. "When Captain said he was going to-night, I was thinking it would take a capful of wind to carry the ship back to sea, but now here's more than a capful."

"Ah, yes," said landlord, "it's to-night he goes true enough, and, mind you, though he treated me handsome over the rent, I'm not sure it's a loss to the village. I don't hold with gentrice who fetch their drink from London instead of helping local traders to get their living."

"But you haven't got any rum like his," I said, to draw him out.

His neck grew red above his collar, and I was afraid I'd gone too far; but after a while he got his breath with a grunt.

"John Simmons," he said, "if you've come down here this windy night to talk a lot of fool's talk, you've wasted a journey."

Well, of course, then I had to smooth him down with praising his rum, and Heaven forgive me for swearing it was better than Captain's. For the like of that rum no living lips have tasted save mine and parson's. But somehow or other I brought landlord round,

and presently we must have a glass of his best
to prove its quality.

"Beat that if you can!" he cried, and we
both raised our glasses to our mouths, only to
stop half-way and look at each other in amaze.
For the wind that had been howling outside
like an outrageous dog had all of a sudden
turned as melodious as the carol-boys of a
Christmas Eve.

"Surely that's not my Martha," whispered
landlord; Martha being his great-aunt that
lived in the loft overhead.

We went to the door, and the wind burst it
open so that the handle was driven clean into
the plaster of the wall. But we didn't think
about that at the time; for over our heads,
sailing very comfortably through the windy
stars, was the ship that had passed the summer
in landlord's field. Her portholes and her
bay-window were blazing with lights, and
there was a noise of singing and fiddling on
her decks. "He's gone," shouted landlord
above the storm, "and he's taken half the
village with him!" I could only nod in
answer, not having lungs like bellows of
leather.

In the morning we were able to measure the strength of the storm, and over and above my pigsty there was damage enough wrought in the village to keep us busy. True it is that the children had to break down no branches for the firing that autumn, since the wind had strewn the woods with more than they could carry away. Many of our ghosts were scattered abroad, but this time very few came back, all the young men having sailed with Captain ; and not only ghosts, for a poor half-witted lad was missing, and we reckoned that he had stowed himself away or perhaps shipped as cabin-boy, not knowing any better.

What with the lamentations of the ghost-girls and the grumblings of families who had lost an ancestor, the village was upset for a while, and the funny thing was that it was the folk who had complained most of the carryings-on of the youngsters, who made most noise now that they were gone. I hadn't any sympathy with shoemaker or butcher, who ran about saying how much they missed their lads, but it made me grieve to hear the poor bereaved girls calling their lovers by name on the village green at nightfall. It didn't seem

fair to me that they should have lost their
men a second time, after giving up life in
order to join them, as like as not. Still, not
even a spirit can be sorry for ever, and after a
few months we made up our mind that the
folk who had sailed in the ship were never·
coming back, and we didn't talk about it any
more.

And then one day, I dare say it would be
a couple of years after, when the whole business was quite forgotten, who should come
trapesing along the road from Portsmouth
but the daft lad who had gone away with the
ship, without waiting till he was dead to become a ghost. You never saw such a boy as
that in all your life. He had a great rusty
cutlass hanging to a string at his waist, and he
was tattooed all over in fine colours, so that
even his face looked like a girl's sampler. He
had a handkerchief in his hand full of foreign
shells and old-fashioned pieces of small money,
very curious, and he walked up to the well
outside his mother's house and drew himself a
drink as if he had been nowhere in particular.

The worst of it was that he had come back
as soft-headed as he went, and try as we

might we couldn't get anything reasonable
out of him. He talked a lot of gibberish
about keel-hauling and walking the plank and
crimson murders—things which a decent sailor
should know nothing about, so that it seemed
to me that for all his manners Captain had
been more of a pirate than a gentleman
mariner. But to draw sense out of that boy
was as hard as picking cherries off a crab-tree.
One silly tale he had that he kept on drifting
back to, and to hear him you would have
thought that it was the only thing that
happened to him in his life. "We was at
anchor," he would say, "off an island called
the Basket of Flowers, and the sailors had
caught a lot of parrots and we were teaching
them to swear. Up and down the decks, up
and down the decks, and the language they
used was dreadful. Then we looked up and
saw the masts of the Spanish ship outside the
harbour. Outside the harbour they were, so
we threw the parrots into the sea and sailed
out to fight. And all the parrots were
drownded in the sea and the language they
used was dreadful." That's the sort of boy he
was, nothing but silly talk of parrots when

we asked him about the fighting. And we never had a chance of teaching him better, for two days after he ran away again, and hasn't been seen since.

That's my story, and I assure you that things like that are happening at Fairfield all the time. The ship has never come back, but somehow as people grow older they seem to think that one of these windy nights she'll come sailing in over the hedges with all the lost ghosts on board. Well, when she comes, she'll be welcome. There's one ghost-lass that has never grown tired of waiting for her lad to return. Every night you'll see her out on the green, straining her poor eyes with looking for the mast-lights among the stars. A faithful lass you'd call her, and I'm thinking you'd be right.

Landlord's field wasn't a penny the worse for the visit, but they do say that since then the turnips that have been grown in it have tasted of rum.

A DRAMA OF YOUTH

I

For some days school had seemed to me even more tedious than usual. The long train journey in the morning, the walk through Farringdon Meat Market, which æsthetic butchers made hideous with mosaics of the intestines of animals, as if the horror of suety pavements and bloody sawdust did not suffice, the weariness of inventing lies that no one believed to account for my lateness and neglected homework, and the monotonous lessons that held me from my dreams without ever for a single instant capturing my interest —all these things made me ill with repulsion. Worst of all was the society of my cheerful, contented comrades, to avoid which I was compelled to mope in deserted corridors, the prey of a sorrow that could not be enjoyed, a hatred that was in no way stimulating. At the best of times the atmosphere of the place disgusted me. Desks, windows, and floors, and even the grass in the quadrangle, were greasy with London soot, and there was nowhere any clean air to breathe or smell. I hated the gritty asphalt that gave no peace to my feet and cut my knees when my clumsiness made me fall. I hated the long stone corridors whose echoes seemed to me to mock my hesitating footsteps when I passed from one dull class to another. I hated the stuffy malodorous class-rooms, with their whistling gas-jets and noise of inharmonious life. I would have hated the yellow fogs had they not sometimes shortened the hours of my bondage. That five hundred boys shared this horrible environment with me did not abate my sufferings a jot ; for it was clear that they did not find it distasteful, and they therefore became as unsympathetic for me as the smell and noise and rotting stones of the school itself.

The masters moved as it were in another world, and, as the classes were large, they understood me as little as I understood them.

They knew that I was idle and untruthful, and
they could not know that I was as full of
nerves as a girl, and that the mere task of
getting to school every morning made me
physically sick. They punished me re-
peatedly and in vain, for I found every hour I
passed within the walls of the school an overwhelming punishment in itself, and nothing
made any difference to me. I lied to them
because they expected it, and because I had
no words in which to express the truth if I
knew it, which is doubtful. For some reason
I could not tell them at home why I got on
so badly at school, or no doubt they would
have taken me away and sent me to a country
school, as they did afterwards. Nearly all the
real sorrows of childhood are due to this
dumbness of the emotions ; we teach children
to convey facts by means of words, but we do
not teach them how to make their feelings in-
telligible. Unfortunately, perhaps, I was very
happy at night with my story-books and
my dreams, so that the real misery of my
days escaped the attention of the grown-up
people. Of course I never even thought of
doing my homework, and the labour of in-

venting new lies every day to account for my negligence became so wearisome that once or twice I told the truth and simply said I had not done it; but the masters held that this frankness aggravated the offence, and I had to take up anew my tiresome tale of improbable calamities. Sometimes my stories were so wild that the whole class would laugh, and I would have to laugh myself; yet on the strength of this elaborate politeness to authority I came to believe myself that I was untruthful by nature.

The boys disliked me because I was not sociable, but after a time they grew tired of bullying me and left me alone. I detested them because they were all so much alike that their numbers filled me with horror. I remember that the first day I went to school I walked round and round the quadrangle in the luncheon-hour, and every boy who passed stopped me and asked me my name and what my father was. When I said he was an engineer every one of the boys replied, "Oh! the man who drives the engine." The reiteration of this childish joke made me hate them from the first, and afterwards I discovered

that they were equally unimaginative in everything they did. Sometimes I would stand in
the midst of them, and wonder what was the
matter with me that I should be so different
from all the rest. When they teased me,
repeating the same questions over and over
again, I cried easily, like a girl, without
quite knowing why, for their stupidities
could not hurt my reason; but when they
bullied me I did not cry, because the pain
made me forget the sadness of my heart.
Perhaps it was because of this that they
thought I was a little mad.

Grey day followed grey day, and I might in
time have abandoned all efforts to be faithful
to my dreams, and achieved a kind of beast-
like submission that was all the authorities
expected of notorious dunces. I might have
taught my senses to accept the evil conditions
of life in that unclean place; I might even
have succeeded in making myself one with
the army of shadows that thronged in the
quadrangle and filled the air with meaningless
noise.

But one evening when I reached home I
saw by the faces of the grown-up people that

something had upset their elaborate pre-
cautions for an ordered life, and I discovered
that my brother, who had stayed at home with
a cold, was ill in bed with the measles. For a
while the significance of the news escaped
me; then, with a sudden movement of my
heart, which made me feel ill, I realised that
probably I would have to stay away from
school because of the infection. My feet
tapped on the floor with joy, though I tried to
appear unconcerned. Then, as I nursed my
sudden hope of freedom, a little fearfully lest
it should prove an illusion, a new and enchant-
ing idea came to me. I slipped from the
room, ran upstairs to my bedroom and, standing by the side of my bed, tore open my
waistcoat and shirt with clumsy, trembling
fingers. One, two, three, four, five! I
counted the spots in a triumphant voice, and
then with a sudden revulsion sat down on the
bed to give the world an opportunity to settle
back in its place. I had the measles, and
therefore I should not have to go back to
school! I shut my eyes for a minute and
opened them again, but still I had the measles.
The cup of happiness was at my lips, but I

sipped delicately because it was full to the brim, and I would not spill a drop.

This mood did not last long. I had to run down the house and tell the world the good news. The grown-up people rebuked my joyousness, while admitting that it might be as well that I should have the measles then as later on. In spite of their air of resignation I could hardly sit still for excitement. I wanted to go into the kitchen and show my measles to the servants, but I was told to stay where I was in front of the fire while my bed was moved into my brother's room. So I stared at the glowing coals till my eyes watered, and dreamed long dreams. I would lie in bed for days, all warm from head to foot, and no one would interrupt my pleasant excursions in the world I preferred to this. If I had heard of the beneficent microbe to which I owed my happiness, I would have mentioned it in my prayers.

Late that night I called over to my brother to ask how long measles lasted. He told me to go to sleep, so that I knew he did not know the answer to my question. I lay at ease tranquilly turning the problem over in my mind. Four weeks, six weeks, eight weeks; why, if I was lucky, it would carry me through to the holidays! At all events, school was already very far away, like a nightmare remembered at noon. I said good-night to my brother, and received an irritated grunt in reply. I did not mind his surliness; tomorrow when I woke up, I would begin my dreams.

II

When I found myself in bed in the morning, already sick at heart because even while I slept I could not forget the long torment of my life at school, I would lie still for a minute or two and try to concentrate my shuddering mind on something pleasant, some little detail of the moment that seemed to justify hope. Perhaps I had some money to spend or a holiday to look forward to ; though often enough I would find nothing to save me from realising with childish intensity the greyness of the world in which it was my fate to move. I did not want to go out into life; it was dull and cruel and greasy with soot. I

only wanted to stop at home in any little
quiet corner out of everybody's way and think
my long, heroic thoughts. But even while I
mumbled my hasty breakfast and ran to the
station to catch my train the atmosphere of
the school was all about me, and my dreamer's
courage trembled and vanished.

When I woke from sleep the morning after
my good fortune, I did not at first realise the
extent of my happiness ; I only knew that
deep in my heart I was conscious of some
great cause for joy. Then my eyes, still dim
with sleep, discovered that I was in my
brother's bedroom, and in a flash the joyful
truth was revealed to me.   I sat up and
hastily examined my body to make sure that
the rash had not disappeared, and then my
spirit sang a song of thanksgiving of which the
refrain was, " I have the measles ! " I lay
back in bed and enjoyed the exquisite luxury
of thinking of the evils that I had escaped.
For once my morbid sense of atmosphere was
a desirable possession and helpful to my happiness.   It was delightful to pull the bedclothes
over my shoulders and conceive the feelings of
a small boy who should ride to town in a

jolting train, walk through a hundred kinds of
dirt and a hundred disgusting smells to win to
prison at last, where he should perform meaningless tasks in the distressing society of five
hundred mocking apes. It was pleasant to
see the morning sun and feel no sickness in
my stomach, no sense of depression in my
tired brain. Across the room my brother
gurgled and choked in his sleep, and in some
subtle way contributed to my ecstasy of tranquillity. I was no longer concerned for the
duration of my happiness. I felt that this
peace that I had desired so long must surely
last for ever.

To the grown-up folk who came to see us
during the day—the doctor, certain germ-
proof unmarried aunts, truculently maternal,
and the family itself—my brother's case was
far more interesting than mine because he had
caught the measles really badly. I just had
them comfortably; enough to be infectious,
but not enough to feel ill, so I was left in
pleasant solitude while the women competed
for the honour of smoothing my brothers'
pillow and tiptoeing in a fidgeting manner
round his bed. I lay on my back and looked

with placid interest at the cracks in the ceiling. They were like the main roads in a map, and I amused myself by building little houses beside them—houses full of books and warm hearthrugs, and with a nice pond lively with tadpoles in the garden of each. From the windows of the houses you could watch all the traffic that went along the road, men and women and horses, and best of all, the boys going to school in the morning—boys who had not done their homework and who would be late for prayers. When I talked about the cracks to my brother he said that perhaps the ceiling would give way and fall on our heads. I thought about this too, and found it quite easy to picture myself lying in the bed with a smashed head, and blood all over the pillow. Then it occurred to me that the plaster might smash me all over, and my impressions of Farringdon Meat Market added a gruesome vividness to my conception of the consequences. I always found it pleasant to imagine horrible things; it was only the reality that made me sick.

Towards nightfall I became a little feverish, and I heard the grown-ups say that they would

give me some medicine later on. Medicine
for me signified the nauseous powders of Dr.
Gregory, so I pretended to be asleep every
time any one came into the room, in order to
escape my destiny, until at last some one
stood by my bedside so long that I became
cramped and had to pretend to wake up.
Then I was given the medicine, and found to
my surprise that it was delicious and tasted of
oranges. I felt that there had been a mistake
somewhere, but my head sat a little heavily on
my shoulders, and I would not trouble to fix
the responsibility. This time I fell asleep in
earnest, and woke in the middle of the night
to find my brother standing by my bed,
making noises with his mouth. I thought
that he had gone mad, and would kill me
perhaps, but after a time he went back to bed
saying all the bad words he knew. The
excitement had made me wide awake, and I
tossed about thinking of the cracked ceiling
above my head. The room was quite dark,
and I could see nothing, so that it might be
bulging over me without my knowing it. I
stood up in bed and stretched up my arm, but
I could not reach the ceiling ; yet when I lay

down again I felt as though it had sunk so far
that it was touching my hair, and I found it
difficult to breathe in such a small space. I
was afraid to move for fear of bringing it
down upon me, and in a short while the pres-
sure upon my body became unbearable, and I
shrieked out for help. Some one came in and
lit the gas, and found me looking very foolish
and my brother delirious. I fell asleep almost
immediately, but was conscious through my
dreams that the gas was still alight and that
they were watching by my brother's bedside.

In the morning he was very ill and I was
no longer feverish, so it was decided to move
me back into my own bedroom. I was
wrapped up in the bedclothes and told to sit
still while the bed was moved. I sat in an
armchair, feeling like a bundle of old clothes,
and looking at the cracks in the ceiling which
seemed to me like roads. I knew that I had
already lost all importance as an invalid, but I
was very happy nevertheless. For from the
window of one of my little houses I was
watching the boys going to school, and my
heart was warm with the knowledge of my
own emancipation. As my legs hung down

from the chair I found it hard to keep my
slippers on my stockingless feet.

III

There followed for me a period of deep and
unbroken satisfaction. I was soon considered
well enough to get up, and I lived pleasantly
between the sofa and the fireside waiting on
my brother's convalescence, for it had been
settled that I should go away with him to the
country for a change of air. I read Dickens
and Dumas in English, and made up long
stories in which I myself played important
but not always heroic parts. By means of
intellectual exercises of this kind I achieved a
tranquillity like that of an old man, fearing
nothing, desiring nothing, regretting nothing.
I no longer reckoned the days or the hours,
content to enjoy a passionless condition of
being that asked no questions and sought
none of me, nor did I trouble to number my
journeys in the world of infinite shadows.
But in that long hour of peace I realised that
in some inexplicable way I was interested in

the body of a little boy, whose hands obeyed
my unspoken wishes, whose legs sprawled
before me on the sofa. I knew that before I
met him, this boy, whose littleness surprised
me, had suffered ill dreams in a nameless
world, and now, worn out with tears and
humiliation and dread of life, he slept, and
while he slept I watched him dispassionately,
as I would have looked at a crippled daddy-
long-legs. To have felt compassion for him
would have disturbed the tranquillity that was
a necessary condition of my existence, so I
contented myself with noticing his presence
and giving him a small part in the pageant of
my dreams. He was not so beautiful as I
wished all my comrades to be, and he was
besides very small; but shadows are amiable
play-friends, and they did not blame him
because he cried when he was teased and did
not cry when he was beaten, or because the
wild unreason of his sorrow made him find
cause for tears in the very fullness of his rare
enjoyment. For the first time in my life it
seems to me I saw this little boy as he was,
squat-bodied, big-headed, thick-lipped, and
with a face swept clean of all emotions save

where his two great eyes glowed with a sulky
fire under exaggerated eyebrows. I noticed
his grimy nails, his soiled collar, his unbrushed
clothes, the patent signs of defeat changing to
utter rout, and from the heights of my great
peace I was not sorry for him. He was like
that, other boys were different, that was all.

And then on a day fear returned to my
heart, and my newly discovered Utopia was
no more. I do not know what chance word
of the grown-up people or what random
thought of mine did the mischief; but of a
sudden I realised that for all my dreaming
I was only separated by a measurable number
of days from the horror of school. Already
I was sick with fear, and in place of my
dreams I distressed myself by visualising the
scenes of the life I dreaded—the Meat
Market, the dusty shadows of the gym-
nasium, the sombre reticence of the great
hall. All that my lost tranquillity had given
me was a keener sense of my own being; my
smallness, my ugliness, my helplessness in the
face of the great cruel world. Before I had
sometimes been able to dull my emotions in
unpleasant circumstances and thus achieve a

dogged calm; now I was horribly conscious of my physical sensations, and, above all, of that deadly sinking in my stomach called fear. I clenched my hands, telling myself that I was happy, and trying to force my mind to pleasant thoughts; but though my head swam with the effort, I continued to be conscious that I was afraid. In the midst of my mental struggles I discovered that even if I succeeded in thinking happy things I should still have to go back to school after all, and the knowledge that thought could not avert calamity was like a bruise on my mind. I pinched my arms and legs, with the idea that immediate pain would make me forget my fears for the future; but I was not brave enough to pinch them really hard, and I could not forget the motive for my action. I lay back on the sofa and kicked the cushions with my feet in a kind of forlorn anger. Thought was no use, nothing was any use, and my stomach was sick, sick with fear. And suddenly I became aware of an immense fatigue that overwhelmed my mind and my body, and made me feel as helpless as a little child. The tears that were always

near my eyes streamed down my face, making
my cheek sore against the wet cushion, and
my breath came in painful, ridiculous gulps.
For a moment I made an effort to control my
grief; and then I gave way utterly, crying
with my whole body like a little child, until,
like a little child, I fell asleep.

When I awoke the room was grey with
dusk, and I sat up with a swaying head, glad
to hide the shame of my foolish swollen face
amongst the shadows. My mouth was still
salt with tears, and I was very thirsty, but
I was always anxious to hide my weakness
from other people, and I was afraid that if
I asked for something to drink they would
see that I had been crying. The fire had
gone out while I slept, and I felt cold and
stiff, but my abandonment of restraint had
relieved me, and my fear was now no more
than a vague unrest. My mind thought
slowly but very clearly. I saw that it was
a pity that I had not been more ill than I
was, for then, like my brother, I should have
gone away for a month instead of a fortnight.
As it was, everybody laughed at me because
I looked so well, and said they did not believe

that I had been ill at all. If I had thought
of it earlier I might have been able to make
myself worse somehow or other, but now it
was too late. When the maid came in and
lit the gas for tea she blamed me for letting
the fire out, and told me that I had a dirty
face. I was glad of the chance to slip away
and wash my burning cheeks in cold water.
When I had finished and dried my face on
the rough towel I looked at myself in the
glass. I looked as if I had been to the
seaside for a holiday, my cheeks were so
red !

That night as I lay sleepless in my bed,
seeking for a cool place between the sheets
in which to rest my hot feet, the sickness of
fear returned to me, and I knew that I was
lost. I shut my eyes tightly, but I could not
shut out the vivid pictures of school life that
my memory had stored up for my torment;
I beat my head against the pillow, but I could
not change my thoughts. I recalled all the
possible events that might interfere with my
return to school, a new illness, a railway accident, even suicide, but my reason would not
accept these romantic issues. I was helpless

before my destiny, and my destiny made me afraid.

And then, perhaps I was half asleep or fond with fear, I leapt out of bed and stood in the middle of the room to meet life and fight it. The hem of my nightshirt tickled my shin and my feet grew cold on the carpet; but though I stood ready with my fists clenched I could see no adversary among the friendly shadows, I could hear no sound but the drumming of the blood against the walls of my head. I got back into bed and pulled the bedclothes about my chilled body. It seemed that life would not fight fair, and being only a little boy and not wise like the grown-up people, I could find no way in which to outwit it.

IV

My growing panic in the face of my imminent return to school spoilt my holiday, and I watched my brother's careless delight in the Surrey pine-woods with keen envy. It seemed to me that it was easy for him to enjoy himself with his month to squander;

and in any case he was a healthy, cheerful boy who liked school well enough when he was there, though of course he liked holidays better. He had scant patience with my moods, and secretly I too thought they were wicked. We had been taught to believe that we alone were responsible for our sins, and it did not occur to me that the causes of my wickedness might lie beyond my control. The beauty of the scented pines and the new green of the bracken took my breath and filled my heart with a joy that changed immediately to overwhelming grief; for I could not help contrasting this glorious kind of life with the squalid existence to which I must return so soon. I realised so fiercely the force of the contrast that I was afraid to make friends with the pines and admire the palm-like beauty of the bracken lest I should increase my subsequent anguish; and I hid myself in dark corners of the woods to fight the growing sickness of my body with the feeble weapons of my panic-stricken mind. There followed moments of bitter sorrow, when I blamed myself for not taking advantage of my hours of freedom,

and I hurried along the sandy lanes in a
desolate effort to enjoy myself before it was
too late.

In spite of the miserable manner in which
I spent my days, the fortnight seemed to pass
with extraordinary rapidity. As the end
approached, the people around me made it
difficult for me to conceal my emotions, the
grown-ups deducing from my melancholy
that I was tired of holidays and would be
glad to get back to school, and my brother
burdening me with idle messages to the other
boys—messages that shattered my hardly
formed hope that school did not really exist.
I stood ever on the verge of tears, and I
dreaded meal-times, when I had to leave my
solitude, lest some turn of the conversation
should set me weeping before them all, and
I should hear once more what I knew very
well myself, that it was a shameful thing for
a boy of my age to cry like a little girl. Yet
the tears were there and the hard lump in my
throat, and I could not master them, though
I stood in the woods while the sun set with
a splendour that chilled my heart, and tried
to drain my eyes dry of their rebellious, bitter

waters. I would choke over my tea and be
rebuked for bad manners.

When the last day came that I had feared
most of all, I succeeded in saying goodbye to
the people at the house where I had stopped,
and in making the mournful train journey
home without disgracing myself. It seemed
as though a merciful stupor had dulled my
senses to a mute acceptance of my purgatory.
I slept in the train, and arrived home so
sleepy that I was allowed to go straight to
bed without comment. For once my body
dominated my mind, and I slipped between
the sheets in an ecstasy of fatigue and fell
asleep immediately.

Something of this rare mood lingered with
me in the morning, and it was not until I
reached the Meat Market that I realised
the extent of my misfortune. I saw the
greasy, red-faced men with their hands and
aprons stained with blood. I saw the hideous
carcases of animals, the masses of entrails, the
heaps of repulsive hides; but most clearly of
all I saw an ugly sad little boy with a satchel
of books on his back set down in the midst of
an enormous and hostile world. The windows

and stones of the houses were black with soot, and before me there lay school, the place that had never brought me anything but sorrow and humiliation. I went on, but as I slid on the cobbles, my mind caught an echo of peace, the peace of pine-woods and heather, the peace of the library at home, and, my body trembling with revulsion, I leant against a lamp-post, deadly sick. Then I turned on my heels and walked away from the Meat Market and the school for ever. As I went I cried, sometimes openly before all men, sometimes furtively before shop-windows, dabbing my eyes with a wet pocket-handkerchief, and gasping for breath. I did not care where my feet led me, I would go back to school no more.

I had played truant for three days before the grown-ups discovered that I had not returned to school. They treated me with that extraordinary consideration that they always extended to our great crimes and never to our little sins of thoughtlessness or high spirits. The doctor saw me. I was told that I would be sent to a country school after the next holidays, and meanwhile I was allowed to return to my sofa and my dreams. I lay there and read Dickens and was very happy. As a rule the cat kept me company, and I was pleased with his placid society, though he made my legs cramped. I thought that I too would like to be a cat.

THE NEW BOY

I

WHEN I left home to go to boarding-school
for the first time 1 did not cry like the little
boys in the story-books, though I had never
been away from home before except to spend
holidays with relatives. This was not due to
any extraordinary self-control on my part, for
I was always ready to shed tears on the most
trivial occasion. But as a fact I had other
things to think about, and did not in the least
realise the significance of my journey. I had
lots of new clothes and more money in my
pocket than I had ever had before, and in the
guard's van at the back of the train there was
a large box that I had packed myself with
jam and potted meat and cake. In this, as
in other matters, I had been aided by the
expert advice of a brother who was himself

at a school in the North, and it was perhaps natural that in the comfortable security of the holidays he should have given me an almost lyrical account of the joys of life at a boarding-school. Moreover, my existence as a day-boy in London had been so unhappy that I was prepared to welcome any change, so at most I felt only a vague unease as to the future.

After I had glanced at my papers, I sat back and stared at my eldest brother, who had been told off to see me safely to school. At that time I did not like him because he seemed to me unduly insistent on his rights, and I could not help wondering at the tactlessness of the grown-up people in choosing him as my travelling companion. With any one else this journey might have been a joyous affair, but there were incidents between us that neither of us would forget, so that I could find nothing better than an awkward politeness with which to meet his strained amiability. He feigned an intense interest in his magazine, while I looked out of window, with one finger in my waistcoat pocket, scratching the comfortable milled edges of my money.

When I saw little farm-houses, forgotten in
the green dimples of the Kentish hills, I
thought that it would be nice to live there
with a room full of story-books, away from
the discomforts and difficulties of life. Like
a cat, I wanted to dream somewhere where I
would not be trodden on, somewhere where
I would be neglected by friends and foes alike.
This was my normal desire, but side by side
with my craving for peace I was aware of a
new and interesting emotion that suggested
the possibility of a life even more agreeable.
The excitement of packing my box with
provender like a sailor who was going on a
long voyage, the unwonted thrill of having a
large sum of money concealed about my
person, and above all the imaginative yarns
of my elder brother, had fired me with the
thought of adventure. His stories had been
filled with an utter contempt for lessons and
a superb defiance of the authorities, and had
ranged from desperate rabbit-shooting parties
on the Yorkshire Wolds to illicit feasts of
Eccles cakes and tinned lobster in moonlit
dormitories. I thought that it would be
pleasant to experience this romantic kind of

life before settling down for good with my
dreams.

The train wandered on and my eldest brother
and I looked at each other constrainedly. He
had already asked me twice whether I had my
ticket, and I realised that he could not think
of any other neutral remark that fitted the
occasion. It occurred to me to say that the
train was slow, but I remembered with a glow
of anger how he had once rubbed a strawberry
in my face because I had taken the liberty of
offering it to one of his friends, and I held my
peace. I had prayed for his death every night
for three weeks after that, and though he was
still alive the knowledge of my unconfessed
and unrepented wickedness prevented me
from being more than conveniently polite.
He thought I was a cheeky little toad and I
thought he was a bully, so we looked at each
other and did not speak. We were both glad,
therefore, when the train pulled up at the
station that bore the name of my new
school.

My first emotion was a keen regret that my
parents had not sent me to a place where the
sun shone. As we sat in the little omnibus

that carried us from the station to the town,
with my precious boxes safely stored on the
roof, we passed between grey fields whose
featureless expanses melted changelessly into
the grey sky overhead. The prospect alarmed
me, for it seemed to me that this was not a
likely world for adventures; nor was I reassured by the sight of the town, whose one
long street of low, old-fashioned houses struck
me as being mean and sordid. I was conscious
that the place had an unpleasant smell, and I
was already driven to thinking of my pocket-
money and my play-box—agreeable thoughts
which I had made up my mind in the train
to reserve carefully for possible hours of un-
happiness. But the low roof of the omnibus
was like a limit to my imagination, and my
body was troubled by the displeasing contact
of the velvet cushions. I was still wondering
why this made my wrists ache, when the
omnibus lurched from the cobbles on to a
gravel drive, and I saw the school buildings
towering all about me like the walls of a
prison. I jumped out and stretched my legs
while the driver climbed down to collect the
fares. He looked at me without a jot of

interest, and I knew that he must have driven
a great many boys from the station to the
school in the course of his life.

A man appeared in shirt-sleeves of grey
flannel and wheeled my boxes away on a little
truck, and after a while a master came down
and showed us, in a perfunctory manner, over
the more presentable quarters of the school.
My brother was anxious to get away, because
he had not been emancipated long enough to
find the atmosphere of dormitories and class-
rooms agreeable. I was naturally interested
in my new environment, but the presence of
the master constrained me, and I was afraid
to speak in front of this unknown man whom
it was my lot to obey, so we were all relieved
when our hurried inspection was over. He
told me that I was at liberty to do what I
pleased till seven o'clock, so I went for a walk
through the town with my brother.

The day was drawing to a chill grey close,
and the town was filled with a clammy mist
tainted with the odour of sewage, due, I afterwards discovered, to the popular abuse of the
little stream that gave the place its name.
Even my brother could not entirely escape

the melancholy influence of the hour and the place, and he was glad to take me into a baker's shop and have tea. By now the illusion of adventure that had reconciled me to leaving home was in a desperate state, and I drank my tea and consumed my cakes without enjoyment. If life was always going to be the same—if in fleeing one misfortune I had merely brought on myself the pain of becoming accustomed to another—I felt sure that my meagre stoicism would not suffice to carry me through with credit. I had failed once, I would fail again. I looked forward with a sinking heart to a tearful and uncomfortable future.

There was only a very poor train service, so my brother had plenty of time to walk back to the station, and it was settled that I should go part of the way with him. As we walked along the white road, that stretched between uniform hedgerows of a shadowy greyness, I saw that he had something on his mind. In this hour of my trial I was willing to forget the past for the sake of talking for a few minutes with some human being whom I knew, but he returned only vague answers to my eager questions. At last he stopped in the middle of the road, and said I had better turn back. I would liked to have walked farther with him, but I was above all things anxious to keep up appearances, so I said goodbye in as composed a voice as I could find. My brother hesitated for a minute; then with a timid glance at heaven he put his hand in his pocket, pulled out half a crown which he gave me, and walked rapidly away. I saw in a flash that for him, too, it had been an important moment; he had tipped his first schoolboy, and henceforth he was beyond all question grown up.

I did not like him, but I watched him disappear in the dusk with a desolate heart. At that moment he stood for a great many things that seemed valuable to me, and I would have given much to have been walking by his side with my face towards home and my back turned to the grey and unsavoury town to which I had to bear my despondent loneliness. Nevertheless I stepped out staunchly enough, in order that my mind should take courage from the example of my body. I thought strenuously of my brother's stories, of my

play-box packed for a voyage, of the money
in my pocket increased now by my eldest
brother's unexpected generosity; and by dint
of these violent mental exercises I had reduced
my mind to a comfortable stupor by the time
I reached the school gates. There I was
overcome by shyness, and although I saw
lights in the form-rooms and heard the voices
of boys, I stood awkwardly in the playground,
not knowing where I ought to go. The mist
in the air surrounded the lights with a halo,
and my nostrils were filled with the acrid
smell of burning leaves.

I had stood there a quarter of an hour
perhaps, when a boy came up and spoke to
me, and the sound of his voice gave me a
shock. I think it was the first time in my
life a boy had spoken kindly to me. He
asked me my name, and told me that it
would be supper-time in five minutes, so that
I could go and sit in the dining-hall and wait.
"You'll be all right, you know," he said, as he
passed on; "they're not a bad lot of chaps."
The revulsion nearly brought on a catastrophe,
for the tears rose to my eyes and I gazed after
him with a swimming head. I had prepared

myself to receive blows and insults with a calm brow, but I had no armour with which to oppose the noble weapons of sympathy and good fellowship. They overcame the stubborn hatred with which I was accustomed to meet life, and left me defenceless. I felt as if I had been face to face with the hero of a dream.

As I sat at supper before a long table decorated with plates of bread-and-butter and cheese I saw my friend sitting at the other end of the room, so I asked the boy next to me to tell me his name. "Oh," he said, looking curiously at my blushes, "you mean old mother F——. He's pious, you know; reads the Bible and funks at games and all that."

There are some things which no self-respecting schoolboy can afford to forgive. I had made up my mind that it was not pleasant to be an Ishmael, that as far as possible I would try to be an ordinary boy at my new school. My experiences in London had taught me caution, and I was anxious not to compromise my position at the outset by making an unpopular friend. So I nodded my head sagely

in reply, and looked at my new-discovered
hero with an air of profound contempt.

II

The days that followed were not so uncomfortable as my first grey impression of the
place had led me to expect. I proved to my
own intense astonishment to be rather good at
lessons, so that I got on well with the masters,
and the boys were kind enough in their careless way. I had plenty of pocket-money, and
though I did not shine at Association football,
for in London I had only watched the big
boys playing Rugby, I was not afraid of being
knocked about, which was all that was expected of a new boy. Most of my embar-
rassments were due to the sensitiveness that
made me dislike asking questions—a weakness
that was always placing me in false positions.
But my efforts to make myself agreeable to
the boys were not unsuccessful, and while I
looked in vain for anything like the romantic
adventures of which my brother had spoken, I
sometimes found myself almost enjoying my
new life.

And then, as the children say in the streets of London, I woke up, and discovered that I was desperately home-sick. Partly no doubt this was due to a natural reaction, but there were other more obvious causes. For one thing my lavish hospitality had exhausted my pocket-money in the first three weeks, and I was ashamed to write home for more so soon. This speedy end to my apparent wealth certainly made it easier for the boys to find out that I was not one of themselves, and they began to look at me askance and leave me out of their conversations. I was made to feel once more that I had been born under a malignant star that did not allow me to speak or act as they did. I had not their common sense, their blunt cheerfulness, their complete lack of sensibility, and while they resented my queerness they could not know how anxious I was to be an ordinary boy. When I saw that they mistrusted me I was too proud to accept the crumbs of their society like poor mother F——, and I withdrew myself into a solitude that gave me far too much time in which to examine my emotions. I found out all the remote corners of the school in which it was

possible to be alone, and when the other boys
went for walks in the fields, I stayed in the
churchyard close to the school, disturbing the
sheep in their meditations among the tomb-
stones, and thinking what a long time it would
be before I was old enough to die.

Now that the first freshness of my new
environment had worn off, I was able to see
my life as a series of grey pictures that repeated themselves day by day. In my mind
these pictures were marked off from each
other by a sound of bells. I woke in the
morning in a bed that was like all the other
beds, and lay on my back listening to the soft
noises of sleep that filled the air with rumours
of healthy boys. The bell would ring and the
dormitory would break into an uproar, splash-
ing of water, dropping of hair-brushes and
shouts of laughter, for these super-boys could
laugh before breakfast. Then we all trooped
downstairs and I forced myself to drink bad
coffee in a room that smelt of herrings. The
next bell called us to chapel, and at intervals
during the morning other bells called us from
one class to another. Dinner was the one
square meal we had during the day, and as it

was always very good, and there was nothing
morbid about my appetite, I looked forward
to it with interest. After dinner we played
football. I liked the game well enough, but
the atmosphere of mud and forlorn grey fields
made me shudder, and as I kept goal I spent
my leisure moments in hardening my æsthetic
impressions. I never see the word football
to-day without recalling the curious sensation
caused by the mud drying on my bare knees.
After football were other classes, classes in
which it was sometimes very hard to keep
awake, for the school was old, and the badly
ventilated class-rooms were stuffy after the
fresh air. Then the bell summoned us to
evening chapel and tea—a meal which we were
allowed to improve with sardines and eggs and
jam, if we had money to buy them or a hamper
from home. After tea we had about two
hours to ourselves and then came preparation,
and supper and bed. Everything was heralded
by a bell, and now and again even in the midst
of lessons I would hear the church-bell tolling
for a funeral.

I think my hatred of bells dated back to
my early childhood, when the village church,

having only three bells, played the first bar
of "Three Blind Mice" a million times every
Sunday evening, till I could have cried for
monotony and the vexation of the thwarted
tune. But at school I had to pay the penalty
for my prejudice every hour of the day.
Especially I suffered at night during preparation, when they rang the curfew on the
church bells at intolerable length, for these
were tranquil hours to which I looked forward eagerly. We prepared our lessons for
the morrow in the Great Hall, and I would
spread my books out on the desk and let
my legs dangle from the form in a spirit
of contentment for the troubled day happily
past. Over my head the gas stars burned
quietly, and all about me I heard the restrained
breathing of comrades, like a noise of flutter-
ing moths. And then, suddenly, the first
stroke of the curfew would snarl through the
air, filling the roof with nasal echoes, and
troubling the quietude of my mind with
insistent vibrations. I derived small satisfaction from cursing William the Conqueror,
who, the history book told me, was responsible
for this ingenious tyranny. The long pauses

between the strokes held me in a state of
strained expectancy until I wanted to howl.
I would look about me for sympathy and
see the boys at their lessons, and the master
on duty reading quietly at his table. The
curfew rang every night, and they did not
notice it at all.

The only bell I liked to hear was the
last bell that called us to our brief supper
and to bed, for once the light was out and
my body was between the sheets I was free
to do what I would, free to think or to
dream or to cry. There was no real difference between being in bed at school or
anywhere else ; and sometimes I would fill
the shadows of the dormitory with the
familiar furniture of my little bedroom at
home, and pretend that I was happy. But
as a rule I came to bed brimming over with
the day's tears, and I would pull the bed-
clothes over my head so that the other boys
should not know that I was homesick, and
cry until I was sticky with tears and
perspiration.

The discipline at school did not make us
good boys, but it made us civilised ; it taught

us to conceal our crimes. And as home-
sickness was justly regarded as a crime of
ingratitude to the authorities and to society
in general, I had to restrain my physical
weakness during the day, and the reaction
from this restraint made my tears at night
almost a luxury. My longing for home was
founded on trifles, but it was not the less
passionate. I hated this life spent in walking
on bare boards, and the blank walls and
polished forms of the school appeared to me
to be sordid. When now and again I went
into one of the master's studies and felt a
carpet under my feet, and saw a pleasant
litter of pipes and novels lying on the table,
it seemed to me that I was in a holy place,
and I looked at the hearthrug, the wallpaper,
and the upholstered chairs with a kind of
desolate love for things that were nice to
see and touch. I suppose that if we had
been in a workhouse, a prison, or a lunatic
asylum, our æsthetic environment would have
been very much the same as it was at school;
and afterwards when I went with the cricket
and football teams to other grammar schools
they all gave me the same impression of clean

ugliness. It is not surprising that few boys
emerge from their school life with that feeling
for colour and form which is common to
nearly all children.

There was something very unpleasant to
me in the fact that we all washed with the
same kind of soap, drank out of the same kind
of cup, and in general did the same things at
the same time. The school time-table robbed
life of all those accidental variations that
make it interesting. Our meals, our games,
even our hours of freedom seemed only like
subtle lessons. We had to eat at a certain
hour whether we were hungry or not, we
had to play at a certain hour when perhaps
we wanted to sit still and be quiet. The
whole school discipline tended to the formation of habits at the expense of our reasoning
faculties. Yet the astonishing thing to me
was that the boys themselves set up standards
of conduct that still further narrowed the
possibilities of our life. It was bad form to
read too much, to write home except on
Sundays, to work outside the appointed
hours, to talk to the day-boys, to cultivate
social relationships with the masters, to be

Cambridge in the boat-race, and in fine to hold any opinion or follow any pursuit that was not approved by the majority. It was only by hiding myself away in corners that I could enjoy any liberty of spirit, and though my thoughts were often cheerless when I remembered the relative freedom of home life, I preferred to linger with them rather than to weary myself in breaking the little laws of a society for which I was in no way fitted.

These were black days, rendered blacker by my morbid fear of the physical weakness that made me liable to cry at any moment, sometimes even without in the least knowing why. I was often on the brink of disaster, but my fear of the boys' ridicule prevented me from publicly disgracing myself. Once the headmaster called a boy into his study, and he came out afterwards with red eyelids and a puffed face. When they heard that his mother had died suddenly in India, all the boys thought that these manifestations of sorrow were very creditable, and in the best of taste, especially as he did not let anybody see him crying. For

my part I looked at him with a kind of
envy, this boy who could flaunt his woe
where he would. I, too, had my unassuage-
able sorrow for the home that was dead
to me those forlorn days; but I could only
express it among the tombs in the churchyard,
or at night, muffled between the blankets,
when the silent dormitory seemed to listen
with suspicious ears.

III

A consoling scrap of wisdom which unfortunately children do not find written large
in their copybooks is that sorrow is as
transitory as happiness. Although my childhood was strewn with the memorial wreaths
of dead miseries, I always had a morbid sense
that my present discomforts were immortal.
So I had quite made up my mind that I
would continue to be unhappy at school,
when the intervention of two beings whom
I had thought utterly remote from me, gave
me a new philosophy and reconciled me to
life. The first was a master, who found me

grieving in one of my oubliettes and took me
into his study and tried to draw me out.
Kindness always made me ineloquent, and
as I sat in his big basket chair and sniffed the
delightful odour of his pipe, I expressed
myself chiefly in woe-begone monosyllables
and hiccoughs. Nevertheless he seemed to
understand me very well, and though he
did not say much, I felt by the way in which
he puffed out great, generous clouds of smoke,
that he sympathised with me. He told me
to come and see him twice a week, and that
I was at liberty to read any of his books,
and in general gave me a sense that I was
unfortunate rather than criminal. This did
me good, because a large part of my unhappi-
ness was due to the fact that constant suppres-
sion by majorities had robbed me of my
self-respect. It is better for a boy to be
conceited than to be ashamed of his own
nature, and to shudder when he sees his face
reflected in a glass.

My second benefactor was nominally a
boy, though in reality he was nearly as old
as the master, and was leaving at the end
of the term to go up to Oxford. He took

me by the shoulder one evening in the
dusk, and walked me round and round the
big clump of rhododendrons that stood in
the drive in front of the school. I did not
understand half he said, but to my great
astonishment I heard him confessing that
he had always been unhappy at school,
although at the end he was captain in lessons,
in games, in everything. I was, of course,
highly flattered that this giant should speak
to me as an equal, and admit me to his
confidences. But I was even more delighted
with the encouraging light he threw on school
life. "You're only here for a little spell,
you know; you'll be surprised how short it
is. And don't be miserable just because
you're different. I'm different; it's a jolly
good thing to be different." I was not used
to people who took this wide view of circumstance, and his voice in the shadows sounded
like some one speaking in a story-book.
Yet although his monologue gave me an
entirely new conception of life, no more of
it lingers in my mind, save his last reflective
criticism. "All the same, I don't see why
you should always have dirty nails." He

never confided in me again, and I would have
died rather than have reminded him of his
kindly indiscretion; but when he passed me
in the playground he seemed to look at
me with a kind of reticent interest, and it
occurred to me that after all my queerness
might not be such a bad thing, might even be
something to be proud of.

The value of this discovery to me can hardly
be exaggerated. Hitherto in my relationships
with the boys I had fought nothing but losing
battles, for I had taken it for granted that
they were right and I was wrong. But now
that I had hit on the astonishing theory that
the individual has the right to think for himself, I saw quite clearly that most of their
standards of conduct sprang from their sheep-
like stupidity. They moved in flocks because
they had not the courage to choose a line for
themselves. The material result of this new
theory of life was to make me enormously
conceited, and I moved among my comrades
with a mysterious confidence, and gave myself
the airs of a Byron in knickerbockers. My
unpopularity increased by leaps and bounds,
but so did my moral courage, and I accepted

the belated efforts of my school-fellows to knock the intelligence out of me as so many tributes to the force of my individuality. I no longer cried in my bed at night, but lay awake enraptured at the profundity of my thoughts. After years of unquestioning humility I enjoyed a prolonged debauch of intellectual pride, and I marvelled at the little boy of yesterday who had wept because he could not be an imbecile. It was the apotheosis of the ugly duckling, and I saw my swan's plumage reflected in the placid faces of the boys around me, as in the vacant waters of a pool. As yet I did not dream of a moulting season, still less that a day would come when I should envy the ducks their domestic ease and the unthinking tranquillity of their lives. A little boy may be excused for not realising that Hans Andersen's story is only the prelude to a sadder story that he had not the heart to write.

My new freedom of spirit gave me courage to re-examine the emotional and æsthetic values of my environment. I could not persuade myself that I liked the sound of bells, and the greyness of the country in

winter-time still revolted me, as though I had
not yet forgotten the cheerful reds and greens
and blues of the picture-books that filled my
mind as a child with dreams of a delightful
world. But now that I was wise enough to
make the best of my unboyish emotionalism,
I began to take pleasure in certain phases of
school-life. Though I was devoid of any
recognisable religious sense I liked the wide
words in the Psalms that we read at night in
the school chapel. This was not due to any
precocious recognition of their poetry, but to
the fact that their intense imagery conjured
up all sorts of precious visions in my mind,
I could see the hart panting after the water-
brooks, in the valleys of Exmoor, where I had
once spent an enchanted holiday. I could see
the men going down to the sea in ships, and
the stormy waves, and the staggering, fearful
mariners, for I had witnessed a great tempest
off Flamborough Head. Even such vague
phrases as " the hills " gave me an intense joy.
I could see them so clearly, those hills, chalky
hills covered with wild pansies, and with an
all-blue sky overhead, like the lid of a choco-
late-box. I liked, too, the services in the old

church on Sunday nights, when the lights
were lowered for the sermon, and I would put
my hands over my ears and hear the voice of
the preacher like the drone of a distant bee.
After church the choral society used to prac-
tise in the Great Hall, and as I walked round
the school buildings, snatches of their singing
would beat against my face like sudden gusts
of wind. When I listened at the doors of my
form-room I heard the boys talking about
football matches, or indulging their tireless
passion for unimaginative personalities; I
would stand on the mat outside wondering
whether I would be allowed to read if I
went in.

I looked forward to Tuesday night, which
was my bath-night, almost as much as to
Sunday. The school sanitary arrangements
were primitive, and all the water had to be
fetched in pails, and I used to like to see the
man tipping the hot water into the bath and
flinging his great body back to avoid the steam
that made his grey flannel shirt-sleeves cling
to his hairy arms. Most of the boys added a
lot of cold water, but I liked to boil myself
because the subsequent languor was so pleasant.

The matron would bring our own bath towels warm from the fire, and I would press mine against my face because it smelt of childhood and of home. I always thought my body looked pretty after a really hot bath; its rosiness enabled me to forgive myself for being fat.

One very strong impression was connected with the only master in the school whom I did not like. He was a German, and as is the case with others of his nationality, a spray of saliva flew from his lips when he was angry, and seeing this, I would edge away from him in alarm. Perhaps it was on this account that he treated me with systematic unfairness and set himself the unnecessary task of making me ridiculous in the eyes of the other boys. One night I was wandering in the playground and heard him playing the violin in his study. My taste in music was barbarian; I liked comic songs, which I used to sing to myself in a lugubrious voice, and in London the plaintive clamour of the street-organs had helped to make my sorrows rhythmical. But now, perhaps for the first time, I became aware of the illimitable melancholy that lies at the heart of all great music. It seemed to me that the

German master, the man whom I hated, had shut himself up alone in his study, and was crying aloud. I knew that if he was unhappy, it must be because he too was an Ishmael, a personality, one of the different ones. A great sympathy woke within me, and I peeped through the window and saw him playing with his face all shiny with perspiration and a silk handkerchief tucked under his chin. I would have liked to have knocked at his door and told him that I knew all about these things, but I was afraid that he would think me cheeky and splutter in my face.

The next day in his class, I looked at him hopefully, in the light of my new understanding, but it did not seem to make any difference. He only told me to get on with my work.

IV

The term drew to a close, and most of the boys in my form-room ticked off the days on lists, in which the Sundays were written in red ink to show that they did not really count. As time went on they grew more and more

boisterous, and wherever I went I heard them
telling one another how they were going to
spend their holidays. It was surprising to me
that these boys who were so ordinary during
term-time should lead such adventurous lives
in the holidays, and I felt a little envious of
their good fortune. They talked of visiting
the theatre and foreign-travel in a matter-of-
fact way that made me think that perhaps
after all my home-life was incomplete. I had
never been out of England, and my dramatic
knowledge was limited to pantomimes, for
which these enthusiastic students of musical
comedy expressed a large contempt. Some
of them were allowed to shoot with real guns
in the holidays, which reminded me of the
worst excesses of my brother in Yorkshire.
Examining my own life, I had often come to
the conclusion that adventures did not exist
outside books. But the boys shook this com-
forting theory with their boastful prophecies,
and I thought once more that perhaps it was
my misfortune that they did not happen to
me. I began to fear that I would find the
holidays tame.

There were other considerations that made

me look forward to the end of the term with misgiving. Since it had been made plain to me that I was a remarkable boy, I had rather enjoyed my life at school. I had conceived myself as strutting with a measured dignity before a background of the other boys —a background that moved and did not change, like a wind-swept tapestry; but I was quite sure that I would not be allowed to give myself airs at home. It seemed to me that a youngest brother's portion of freedom would compare but poorly with the measure of intellectual liberty that I had secured for myself at school. My brothers were all very well in their way, but I would be expected to take my place in the background and do what I was told. I should miss my sense of being superior to my environment, and my intensely emotional Sundays would no longer divide time into weeks. The more I thought of it, the more I realised that I did not want to go home.

On the last night of the term, when the dormitory had at length become quiet, I considered the whole case dispassionately in my bed. The labour of packing my play-box and writing labels for my luggage had given me a momentary thrill, but for the rest I had moved among my insurgent comrades with a chilled heart. I knew now that I was too greedy of life, that I always thought of the pleasant side of things when they were no longer within my grasp; but at the same time my discontent was not wholly unreasonable. I had learnt more of myself in three months than I had in all my life before, and from being a nervous, hysterical boy I had arrived at a complete understanding of my emotions, which I studied with an almost adult calmness of mind. I knew that in returning to the society of my healthy, boyish brothers, I was going back to a kind of life for which I was no longer fitted. I had changed, but I had the sense to see that it was a change that would not appeal to them, and that in consequence I would have another and harder battle to fight before I was allowed to go my own way.

I saw further still. I saw that after a month at home I would not want to come back to school, and that I should have to endure another period of despondency. I

saw that my whole school life would be
punctuated by these violent uprootings, that
the alternation of term-time and holidays
would make it impossible for me to change life
into a comfortable habit, and that even to the
end of my school-days it would be necessary
for me to preserve my new-found courage.

As I lay thinking in the dark I was proud
of the clarity of my mind, and glad that I
had at last outwitted the tears that had
made my childhood so unhappy. I heard
the boys breathing softly around me—those
wonderful boys who could sleep even when
they were excited—and I felt that I was
getting the better of them in thinking while
they slept. I remembered the prefect who
had told me that we were there only for a
little spell, but I did not speculate as to
what would follow afterwards. All that I had
to do was to watch myself ceaselessly, and be
able to explain to myself everything that I felt
and did. In that way I should always be strong
enough to guard my weaknesses from the eyes
of the jealous world in which I moved.

The church bells chimed the hour, and I
turned over and went to sleep.

ON THE BRIGHTON ROAD

Slowly the sun had climbed up the hard white downs, till it broke with little of the mysterious ritual of dawn upon a sparkling world of snow. There had been a hard frost during the night, and the birds, who hopped about here and there with scant tolerance of life, left no trace of their passage on the silver pavements. In places the sheltered caverns of the hedges broke the monotony of the whiteness that had fallen upon the coloured earth, and overhead the sky melted from orange to deep blue, from deep blue to a blue so pale that it suggested a thin paper screen rather than illimitable space. Across the level fields there came a cold, silent wind which blew fine dust of snow from the trees, but hardly stirred the crested hedges. Once above the sky-line, the sun seemed to climb more quickly, and as it rose higher it began to give out a heat that blended with the keenness of the wind.

It may have been this strange alternation of heat and cold that disturbed the tramp in his dreams, for he struggled for a moment with the snow that covered him, like a man who finds himself twisted uncomfortably in the bed-clothes, and then sat up with staring, questioning eyes. "Lord! I thought I was in bed," he said to himself as he took in the vacant landscape, "and all the while I was out here." He stretched his limbs, and, rising carefully to his feet, shook the snow off his body. As he did so the wind set him shivering, and he knew that his bed had been warm.

"Come, I feel pretty fit," he thought. "I suppose I am lucky to wake at all in this. Or unlucky—it isn't much of a business to come back to." He looked up and saw the downs shining against the blue like the Alps on a picture-postcard. "That means another forty miles or so, I suppose," he continued grimly. "Lord knows what I did yesterday. Walked till I was done, and now I'm only about twelve miles from Brighton.

Damn the snow, damn Brighton, damn everything!" The sun crept up higher and higher, and he started walking patiently along the road with his back turned to the hills.

"Am I glad or sorry that it was only sleep that took me, glad or sorry, glad or sorry?" His thoughts seemed to arrange themselves in a metrical accompaniment to the steady thud of his footsteps, and he hardly sought an answer to his question. It was good enough to walk to.

Presently, when three milestones had loitered past, he overtook a boy who was stooping to light a cigarette. He wore no overcoat, and looked unspeakably fragile against the snow. "Are you on the road, guv'nor?" asked the boy huskily as he passed.

"I think I am," the tramp said.

"Oh! then I'll come a bit of the way with you if you don't walk too fast. It's a bit lonesome walking this time of day." The tramp nodded his head, and the boy started limping along by his side.

"I'm eighteen," he said casually. "I bet you thought I was younger."

"Fifteen, I'd have said."

"You'd have backed a loser. Eighteen last August, and I've been on the road six years. I ran away from home five times when I was a little 'un, and the police took me back each time. Very good to me, the police was. Now I haven't got a home to run away from."

"Nor have I," the tramp said calmly.

"Oh, I can see what you are," the boy panted; "you're a gentleman come down. It's harder for you than for me." The tramp glanced at the limping, feeble figure and lessened his pace.

"I haven't been at it as long as you have," he admitted.

"No, I could tell that by the way you walk. You haven't got tired yet. Perhaps you expect something the other end?"

The tramp reflected for a moment. "I don't know," he said bitterly, "I'm always expecting things."

"You'll grow out of that," the boy commented. "It's warmer in London, but it's harder to come by grub. There isn't much in it really."

"Still, there's the chance of meeting somebody there who will understand——"

"Country people are better," the boy interrupted. "Last night I took a lease of a barn for nothing and slept with the cows, and this morning the farmer routed me out and gave me tea and toke because I was little. Of course, I score there; but in London, soup on the Embankment at night, and all the rest of the time coppers moving you on."

"I dropped by the roadside last night and slept where I fell. It's a wonder I didn't die," the tramp said. The boy looked at him sharply.

"How do you know you didn't?" he said.

"I don't see it," the tramp said, after a pause.

"I tell you," the boy said hoarsely, "people like us can't get away from this sort of thing if we want to. Always hungry and thirsty and dog-tired and walking all the time. And yet if any one offers me a nice home and work my stomach feels sick. Do I look strong? I know I'm little for my age, but I've been knocking about like this for six years, and do you think I'm not dead? I was drowned bathing at Margate, and I was killed by a gipsy with a spike—he knocked my head right in; and twice I was froze like you last night; and a motor cut me down on this very road, and yet I'm walking along here now, walking to London to walk away from it again, because I can't help it. Dead! I tell you we can't get away if we want to."

The boy broke off in a fit of coughing, and the tramp paused while he recovered.

"You'd better borrow my coat for a bit, Tommy," he said, "your cough's pretty bad."

"You go to hell!" the boy said fiercely, puffing at his cigarette; "I'm all right. I was telling you about the road. You haven't got down to it yet, but you'll find out presently. We're all dead, all of us who're on it, and we're all tired, yet somehow we can't leave it. There's nice smells in the summer, dust and hay and the wind smack in your face on a hot day; and it's nice waking up in the wet grass on a fine morning. I don't know, I don't know——" he lurched forward suddenly, and the tramp caught him in his arms.

"I'm sick," the boy whispered—"sick."

The tramp looked up and down the road, but he could see no houses or any sign of help. Yet even as he supported the boy doubtfully in the middle of the road a motor-car suddenly flashed in the middle distance, and came smoothly through the snow.

"What's the trouble?" said the driver quietly as he pulled up. "I'm a doctor." He looked at the boy keenly and listened to his strained breathing.

"Pneumonia," he commented. "I'll give him a lift to the infirmary, and you, too, if you like."

The tramp thought of the workhouse and shook his head. "I'd rather walk," he said.

The boy winked faintly as they lifted him into the car.

"I'll meet you beyond Reigate," he murmured to the tramp. "You'll see." And the car vanished along the white road.

All the morning the tramp splashed through the thawing snow, but at midday he begged some bread at a cottage door and crept into a lonely barn to eat it. It was warm in there, and after his meal he fell asleep among the hay. It was dark when he woke, and started trudging once more through the slushy roads.

Two miles beyond Reigate a figure, a fragile figure, slipped out of the darkness to meet him.

" On the road, guv'nor ? " said a husky voice. " Then I'll come a bit of the way with you if you don't walk too fast. It's a bit lonesome walking this time of day."

" But the pneumonia ! " cried the tramp aghast.

" I died at Crawley this morning," said the boy.

A TRAGEDY IN LITTLE

I

JACK, the postmaster's little son, stood in the bow-window of the parlour and watched his mother watering the nasturtiums in the front garden. A certain intensity of purpose was expressed by the manner in which she handled the water-pot. For though it was a fine afternoon the carrier's man had called over the hedge to say that there would be a thunderstorm during the night, and every one knew that he never made a mistake about the weather. Nevertheless, Jack's mother watered the plants as if he had not spoken, for it seemed to her that this mete- orological gift smacked a little of sorcery and black magic ; but in spite of herself she felt sure that there would be a thunderstorm and that her labour was therefore vain, save

perhaps as a protest against idle superstition.
It was in the same spirit that she carried an
umbrella on the brightest summer day.

Jack had been sent indoors because he
would get his legs in the way of the watering-pot in order to cool them, so now he
had to be content to look on, with his nose
pressed so tightly against the pane that from
outside it looked like the base of a sea-
anemone growing in a glass tank. He could
no longer hear the glad chuckle of the
watering-pot when the water ran out, but,
on the other hand, he could write his name
on the window with his tongue, which he
could not have done if he had been in the
garden. Also he had some sweets in his
pocket, bought with a halfpenny stolen from
his own money-box, and as the window did
not taste very nice he slipped one into his
mouth and sucked it with enjoyment. He
did not like being in the parlour, because
he had to sit there with his best clothes on
every Sunday afternoon and read the parish
magazine to his sleepy parents. But the front
window was lovely, like a picture, and, indeed,
he thought that his mother, with the flowers

all about her and the red sky overhead, was
like a lady on one of the beautiful calendars
that the grocer gave away at Christmas
He finished his sweet and started another ;
he always meant to suck them right through
to make them last longer, but when the
sweet was half finished he invariably crunched
it up. His father had done the same thing
as a boy.

The room behind him was getting dark,
but outside the sky seemed to be growing
lighter, and mother still stooped from bed
to bed, moving placidly, like a cow. Sometimes she put the watering-pot down on the
gravel path, and bent to uproot a microscopic
weed or to pull the head off a dead flower.
Sometimes she went to the well to get some
more water, and then Jack was sorry that he
had been shut indoors, for he liked letting the
pail down with a run and hearing it bump
against the brick sides. Once he tapped
upon the window for permission to come
out, but mother shook her head vigorously
without turning round ; and yet his stockings
were hardly wet at all.

Suddenly mother straightened herself, and

Jack looked up and saw his father leaning over the gate. He seemed to be making grimaces, and Jack made haste to laugh aloud in the empty room, because he knew that he was good at seeing his father's jokes. Indeed it was a funny thing that father should come home early from work and make faces at mother from the road. Mother, too, was willing to join in the fun, for she knelt down among the wet flowers, and as her head drooped lower and lower it looked, for one ecstatic moment, as though she were going to turn head over heels. But she lay quite still on the ground, and father came half-way through the gate, and then turned and ran off down the hill towards the station. Jack stood in the window, clapping his hands and laughing ; it was a strange game, but not much harder to understand than most of the amusements of the grown-up people.

And then as nothing happened, as mother did not move and father did not come back, Jack grew frightened. The garden was queer and the room was full of darkness, so he beat on the window to change the game. Then, since mother did not shake her head, he ran

out into the garden, smiling carefully in case
he was being silly. First he went to the gate,
but father was quite small far down the road,
so he turned back and pulled the sleeve of
his mother's dress, to wake her. After a
dreadful while mother got up off the ground
with her skirt all covered with wet earth.
Jack tried to brush it off with his hands and
made a mess of it, but she did not seem to
notice, looking across the garden with such a
desolate face that when he saw it he burst
into tears. For once mother let him cry
himself out without seeking to comfort him;
when he sniffed dolefully, his nostrils were
full of the scent of crushed marigolds. He
could not help watching her hands through
his tears; it seemed as though they were
playing together at cat's-cradle; they were
not still for a moment. But it was her face
that at once frightened and interested him.
One minute it looked smooth and white as
if she was very cross, and the next minute
it was gathered up in little folds as if she was
going to sneeze. Deep down in him something chuckled, and he jumped for fear that
the cross part of her had heard it. At

intervals during the evening, while mother was getting him his supper, this chuckle returned to him, between unnoticed fits of crying. Once she stood holding a plate in the middle of the room for quite five minutes, and he found it hard to control his mirth. If father had been there they would have had good fun together, teasing mother, but by himself he was not sure of his ground. And father did not come back, and mother did not seem to hear his questions.

He had some tomatoes and rice-pudding for his supper, and as mother left him to help himself to brown sugar he enjoyed it very much, carefully leaving the skin of the rice-pudding to the last, because that was the part he liked best. After supper he sat nodding at the open window, looking out over the plum-trees to the sky beyond, where the black clouds were putting out the stars one by one. The garden smelt stuffy, but it was nice to be allowed to sit up when you felt really sleepy. On the whole he felt that it had been a pleasant, exciting sort of day, though once or twice mother had frightened him by looking so strange.

There had been other mysterious days in his
life, however; perhaps he was going to have
another little dead sister. Presently he discovered that it was delightful to shut your
eyes and nod your head and pretend that
you were going to sleep; it was like being
in a swing that went up and up and never
came down again. It was like being in a
rowing-boat on the river after a steamer had
gone by. It was like lying in a cradle under
a lamplit ceiling, a cradle that rocked gently
to and fro while mother sang far-away songs.

He was still a baby when he woke up, and
he slipped off his chair and staggered blindly
across the room to his mother, with his
knuckles in his eyes like a little, little boy.
He climbed into her lap and settled himself
down with a grunt of contentment. There
was a mutter of thunder in his ears, and he
felt great warm drops of rain falling on his
face. And into his dreams he carried the
dim consciousness that the thunderstorm had
begun.

II

The next morning at breakfast-time father

had not come back, and mother said a lot
of things that made Jack feel very uncomfortable. She herself had taught him that any
one who said bad things about his father was
wicked, but now it seemed that she was trying
to tell him something about father that was
not nice. She spoke so slowly that he hardly
understood a word she said, though he
gathered that father had stolen something,
and would be put in prison if he was caught.
With a guilty pang he remembered his own
dealings with his money-box, and he determined to throw away the rest of the sweets
when nobody was looking. Then mother
made the astounding statement that he was
not to go to school that day, but his sudden
joy was checked a little when she said he
was not to go out at all, except into the
back garden. It seemed to Jack that he
must be ill, but when he made this suggestion
to mother, she gave up her explanations with
a sigh. Afterwards she kept on saying aloud,
" I must think, I must think ! " She said it
so often that Jack started keeping count
on his fingers.

The day went slowly enough, for the

garden was wet after the thunderstorm, and
mother would not play any games. Just
before tea-time two gentlemen called and
talked to mother in the parlour, and after
a while they sent for Jack to answer some
questions about father, though mother was
there all the time. They seemed nice gentlemen, but mother did not ask them to stop
to tea, as Jack expected. He thought that
perhaps she was sorry that she had not done
so, for she was very sad all tea-time, and
let him spread his own bread and jam.
When tea was over things were very dull,
and at last Jack started crying because there
was nothing else to do. Presently he heard
a little noise and found that mother was
crying as well. This seemed to him so extraordinary that he stopped crying to watch
her; the tears ran down her cheeks very
quickly, and she kept on wiping them away
with her handkerchief, but if she held her
handkerchief to her eyes perhaps they would
not be able to come out at all. It occurred
to him that possibly she was sorry she had
said wicked things about father, and to
comfort her, for it made him feel fidgety to

see her cry, he whispered to her that he would not tell. But she stared at him hopelessly through her red eyelids, and he felt that he had not said the right thing. She called him her poor boy, and yet it appeared that he was not ill. It was all very mysterious and uncomfortable, and it would be a good thing when father came back and everything went on as before, even though he had to go back to school.

Later on the woman from the mill came in to sit with mother. She brought Jack some sweets, but instead of playing with him she burst into tears. She made more noise when she cried than mother; in fact he was afraid that in a minute he would have to laugh at her snortings, so he went into the parlour and sat there in the dark, eating his sweets, and knitting his brow over the complexities of life. He could see five stars, and there was a light behind the red curtain of the front bedroom at Arber's farm. It was about twelve times as large as a star, and a much prettier colour. By nearly closing his eyes he could see everything double, so that there were ten stars and two

red lights ; he was trying to make everything
come treble when the gate clicked and he
saw his father's shadow. He was delighted
with this happy end to a tiresome day, and
as he ran through the passage he called out
to mother to say that father was back.
Mother did not answer, but he heard a bit
of noise in the kitchen as he opened the front
door.

He said " Good evening " in the grown-up
voice that father encouraged, but father
slipped in and shut the door without saying
a word. Every night when he came back
from the post-office he brought Jack the
gummed edgings off the sheets of stamps,
and Jack held out his hand for them as a
matter of course. Automatically father felt
in his overcoat pocket and pulled out a great
handful. " Take care of them, they're the
last you'll get," he said ; but when Jack asked
why, his father looked at him with the same
hopeless expression that he had found in his
mother's eyes a short while before. Jack felt
a little cross that every one should be so
stupid.

When they went into the kitchen every-

body looked very strange, and Jack sat down
in the corner and listened for an explanation.
As a rule the conversation of the grown-up
people did not amuse him, but to-night he
felt that something had happened, and that
if he kept quiet he might find out what it
was. He had noticed before that when the
grown-ups talked they always said the same
things over and over again, and now they
were worse than usual. Father said, "It's
no good, I've got to go through it;" the
mill-woman said, "Whatever made you do
it, George?" And mother said, "Nothing
will ever happen to me again!" They all
went on saying these things till Jack grew
tired of listening, and started plaiting his
stamp-paper into a mat. If you did it very
neatly it was almost as good as an ordinary
sheet of paper by the time you had finished.
By and by, while he was still at work, the
mill-woman brought him his supper on a
plate, and raising his head he saw that father
and mother were sitting close together,
looking at each other, and saying nothing
at all. He was very disappointed that
although father had come home they had

not had any jokes all the evening, and as
they were all so dull he did not very much
mind being sent to bed when he had finished
his supper. When he said good-night to
father, he noticed that his boots were very
muddy, as if he had walked a long way like
a common postman. He made a joke about
this, but they all looked at him as if he
had said something wrong, so he hurried out
of the room, glad to get away from these
people whose looks had no reasonable significance, and whose words had no discoverable
meaning. It had been a bad day, and he
hoped mother would let him go back to
school the next morning.

And yet though he took off his clothes and
got into bed, the day was not quite over. He
had only dozed for a few minutes when he
was roused by a noise down below, and slip-
ping out on to the staircase he heard the
mill-woman saying good-night in the passage.
When she had gone and the door had banged
behind her, he listened still, and heard his
mother crying and his father talking on and
on in a strange, hoarse voice. Somehow these
incomprehensible sounds made him feel lonely

and he would have liked to have gone downstairs and sat on his mother's lap and blinked
drowsily in his father's face, as he had done
often enough before. But he was always shy
in the presence of strangers, and he felt that
he did not know this woman who wept and
this man who did not laugh. His father was
his play-friend, the sharer of all his fun ; his
mother was a quiet woman who sat and sewed,
and sometimes told them not to be silly,
which was the best joke of all. It was not
right for people to alter. But the thought of
his bedroom made him desolate, and at last he
plucked up his courage, and crept downstairs
on bare feet. Father and mother had gone
back into the kitchen, and he peeped through
the crack of the door to see what they were
doing. Mother was still crying, always crying, but he had to change his position before
he could see father. Then he turned on his
heels and ran upstairs trembling with fear and
disgust. For father, the man of all the jokes,
the man of whom burglars were afraid and
compared with whom all other little boys'
fathers were as dirt, was crying like a little
girl.

He jumped into bed and pulled the bed-clothes over his face to shut out the ugliness of the world.

III

When Jack woke up the next morning he found that the room was full of sunshine, and that father was standing at the end of the bed. The moment Jack opened his eyes, he began telling him something in a serious voice, which was alone sufficient to prevent Jack from understanding what he said. Besides, he used a lot of long words, and Jack thought that it was silly to use long words before breakfast, when nobody could be expected to remember what they meant. Father's body neatly fitted the square of the window, and the sunbeams shone in all round it and made it look splendid ; and if Jack had not already forgotten the unfortunate impression of the night before, this would have enabled him to overcome it. Every now and then father stopped to ask him if he understood, and he said he did, hoping to find out what it was all about later on. It seemed, however, that father was

not going to the post-office any more, and this
caused Jack to picture a series of delightfully
amusing days. When father had finished
talking he appeared to expect Jack to say
something, but Jack contented himself with
trying to look interested, for he knew that
it was always very stupid of little boys not
to understand things they didn't understand.
In reality he felt as if he had been listening
while his father argued aloud with himself,
talking up and down like an earthquake
map.

At breakfast they were still subdued, but
afterwards, as the morning wore on, father
became livelier and helped Jack to build a hut
in the back garden. They built it of bean-
sticks against the wall at the end, and father
broke up a packing-case to get planks for the
roof. Only mother still had a sad face, and
it made Jack angry with her, that she should
be such a spoil-fun. After dinner, while Jack
was playing in the hut, Mr. Simmons, of the
police-station, and another gentleman called
to take father for a walk, and Jack went down
to the front to see them off. Jack knew Mr.
Simmons very well; he had been to tea with

his little boy, but though he thought him a fine sort of man he could not help feeling proud of his father when he saw them side by side. Mr. Simmons looked as if he were ashamed of himself, while father walked along with square shoulders and a high head as if he had just done something splendid. The other gentleman looked like nothing at all beside father.

When they were out of sight Jack went into the house and found mother crying in the kitchen. As he felt more tolerant in his after-dinner mood, he tried to cheer her up by telling her how fine father had looked beside the other two men. Mother raised her face, all swollen and spoilt with weeping, and gazed at her son in astonishment. "They are taking him to prison," she wailed, "and God knows what will become of us."

For a moment Jack felt alarmed. Then a thought came to him and he smiled, like a little boy who has just found a new and delightful game. "Never mind, mother," he said, "we'll help him to escape."

But mother would not stop crying.

SHEPHERD'S BOY

THE path climbed up and up and threatened to
carry me over the highest point of the downs
till it faltered before a sudden outcrop of chalk
and swerved round the hill on the level. I was
grateful for the respite, for I had been walking
all day and my knapsack was growing heavy.
Above me in the blue pastures of the skies
the cloud-sheep were grazing, with the sun on
their snowy backs, and all about me the grey
sheep of earth were cropping the wild pansies
that grew wherever the chalk had won a
covering of soil.

Presently I came upon the shepherd standing erect by the path, a tall, spare man with a
face that the sun and the wind had robbed of
all expression. The dog at his feet looked more
intelligent than he. " You've come up from
the valley," he said as I passed ; " perhaps
you'll have seen my boy ? "

" I'm sorry, I haven't," I said, pausing.

" Sorrow breaks no bones," he muttered, and strode away with his dog at his heels. It seemed to me that the dog was apologetic for his master's rudeness.

I walked on to the little hill-girt village, where I had made up my mind to pass the night. The man at the village shop said he would put me up, so I took off my knapsack and sat down on a sackful of cattle cake while the bacon was cooking.

" If you came over the hill, you'll have met shepherd," said the man, " and he'll have asked you for his boy."

" Yes, but I hadn't seen him."

The shopman nodded. " There are clever folk who say you can see him, and clever folk who say you can't. The simple ones like you and me, we say nothing, but we don't see him. Shepherd hasn't got no boy."

" What! is it a joke ? "

" Well, of course it may be," said the shopman guardedly, " though I can't say I've heard many people laughing at it yet. You see, shepherd's boy he broke his neck. . . .

" That was in the days before they built the

fence above the big chalk-pit that you passed
on your left coming down. A dangerous
place it used to be for the sheep, so shepherd's
boy he used to lie along there to stop them
dropping into it, while shepherd's dog he
stopped them from going too far. And shepherd he used to come down here and have his
glass, for he took it then like you or me.
He's blue ribbon now.

"It was one night when the mists were out
on the hills, and maybe shepherd had had a
glass too much, or maybe he got a bit lost in
the smoke. But when he went up there to
bring them home, he starts driving them into
the pit as straight as could be. Shepherd's
boy he hollered out and ran to stop them, but
four-and-twenty of them went over, and the
lad he went with them. You mayn't believe
me, but five of them weren't so much as
scratched, though it's a sixty feet drop.
Likely they fell soft on top of the others.
But shepherd's boy he was done.

"Shepherd he's a bit spotty now, and most
times he thinks the boy's still with him. And
there are clever folk who'll tell you that
they've seen the boy helping shepherd's dog

with the sheep.   That would be a ghost now,
I shouldn't wonder.   I've never seen it, but
then I'm simple, as you might say.

"But I've had two boys myself, and it seems
to me that a boy like that, who didn't eat and
didn't get into mischief, and did his work,
would be the handiest kind of boy to have
about the place."

THE PASSING OF EDWARD

I FOUND Dorothy sitting sedately on the beach, with a mass of black seaweed twined in her hands and her bare feet sparkling white in the sun. Even in the first glow of recognition I realised that she was paler than she had been the summer before, and yet I cannot blame myself for the tactlessness of my question.

" Where's Edward ? " I said ; and I looked about the sands for a sailor suit and a little pair of prancing legs.

While I looked, Dorothy's eyes watched mine inquiringly, as if she wondered what I might see.

" Edward's dead," she said simply. " He died last year, after you left."

For a moment I could only gaze at the child in silence, and ask myself what reason there was in the thing that had hurt her so.

Now that I knew that Edward played with her no more, I could see that there was a shadow upon her face too dark for her years, and that she had lost, to some extent, that exquisite carelessness of poise which makes children so young. Her voice was so calm that I might have thought her forgetful had I not seen an instant of patent pain in her wide eyes.

"I'm sorry," I said at length, "very, very, sorry indeed. I had brought down my car to take you for a drive, as I promised."

"Oh! Edward *would* have liked that," she answered thoughtfully; "he was so fond of motors."

She swung round suddenly and looked at the sands behind her with staring eyes.

"I thought I heard——" She broke off in confusion.

I, too, had believed for an instant that I had heard something that was not the wind or the distant children or the smooth sea hissing along the beach. During that golden summer which linked me with the dead, Edward had been wont, in moments of elation, to puff up and down the sands, in artistic representation of a nobby, noisy motor-car. But the dead

may play no more, and there was nothing
there but the sands and the hot sky and
Dorothy.

"You had better let me take you for a run,
Dorothy," I said. "The man will drive, and
we can talk as we go along."

She nodded gravely, and began pulling on
her sandy stockings.

"It did not hurt him," she said incon-
sequently.

The restraint in her voice pained me like a
blow.

"Oh, don't, dear, don't!" I cried. "There
is nothing to do but forget."

"I have forgotten, quite," she answered,
pulling at her shoe-laces with calm fingers.
"It was ten months ago."

We walked up to the front, where the car
was waiting, and Dorothy settled herself
among the cushions with a little sigh of contentment, the human quality of which brought
me a certain relief. If only she would laugh
or cry! I sat down by her side, but the man
waited by the open door.

"What is it?" I asked.

"I'm sorry, sir," he answered, looking about

him in confusion, "I thought I saw a young gentleman with you."

He shut the door with a bang, and in a minute we were running through the town. I knew that Dorothy was watching my face with her wounded eyes; but I did not look at her until the green fields leapt up on either side of the white road.

"It is only for a little while that we may not see him," I said ; "all this is nothing."

"I have forgotten," she repeated. "I think this is a very nice motor."

I had not previously complained of the motor, but I was wishing then that it would cease its poignant imitation of a little dead boy, a boy who would play no more. By the touch of Dorothy's sleeve against mine I knew that she could hear it too. And the miles flew by, green and brown and golden, while I wondered what use I might be in the world, who could not help a child to forget. Possibly there was another way, I thought.

"Tell me how it happened," I said.

Dorothy looked at me with inscrutable eyes, and spoke in a voice without emotion.

"He caught a cold, and was very ill in bed.

I went in to see him, and he was all white
and faded. I said to him, 'How are you
Edward?' and he said, 'I shall get up early
in the morning to catch beetles.' I didn't see
him any more."

"Poor little chap!" I murmured.

"I went to the funeral," she continued
monotonously. "It was very rainy, and I
threw a little bunch of flowers down into the
hole. There was a whole lot of flowers there ;
but I think Edward liked apples better than
flowers."

"Did you cry?" I said cruelly.

She paused. "I don't know. I suppose
so. It was a long time ago; I think I have
forgotten."

Even while she spoke I heard Edward
puffing along the sands: Edward who had
been so fond of apples.

"I cannot stand this any longer," I said
aloud. "Let's get out and walk in the woods
for a change."

She agreed, with a depth of comprehension
that terrified me ; and the motor pulled up
with a jerk at a spot where hardly a post
served to mark where the woods commenced

and the wayside grass stopped. We took one of the dim paths which the rabbits had made and forced our way through the undergrowth into the peaceful twilight of the trees.

"You haven't got very sunburnt this year," I said as we walked.

"I don't know why. I've been out on the beach all the days. Sometimes I've played, too."

I did not ask her what games she had played, or who had been her play-friend. Yet even there in the quiet woods I knew that Edward was holding her back from me. It is true that, in his boy's way, he had been fond of me; but I should not have dared to take her out without him in the days when his live lips had filled the beach with song, and his small brown body had danced among the surf. Now it seemed that I had been disloyal to him.

And presently we came to a clearing where the leaves of forgotten years lay brown and rotten beneath our feet, and the air was full of the dryness of death.

"Let's be going back. What do you think, Dorothy?" I said.

" I think," she said slowly,—" I think that this would be a very good place to catch beetles."

A wood is full of secret noises, and that is why, I suppose, we heard a pair of small quick feet come with a dance of triumph through the rustling bracken. For a minute we listened deeply, and then Dorothy broke from my side with a piercing call on her lips.

" Oh, Edward, Edward ! " she cried ; " Edward ! "

But the dead may play no more, and presently she came back to me with the tears that are the riches of childhood streaming down her face.

" I can hear him, I can hear him," she sobbed ; " but I cannot see him. Never, never again."

And so I led her back to the motor. But in her tears I seemed to find a promise of peace that she had not known before.

Now Edward was no very wonderful little boy ; it may be that he was jealous and vain and greedy ; yet now, it seemed as he lay in his small grave with the memory of Dorothy's flowers about him, he had wrought this kindness for his sister. Yes, even though we heard no more than the birds in the branches and the wind swaying the scented bracken; even though he had passed with another summer, and the dead and the love of the dead may rise no more from the grave.

THE STORY OF A BOOK

I. THE WRITER

THE history of a book must necessarily begin with the history of its author, for surely in these enlightened days neither the youngest nor the oldest of critics can believe that works of art are found under gooseberry-bushes or in the nests of storks. In truth, I am by no means sure that everybody knew this before the publication of "The Man Shakespeare," and for the sake of a mystified posterity it may be well to explain that there was once a school of criticism that thought it indecent to pry into that treasure-house of individuality from which, if we reject the nursery hypotheses mentioned above, it is clearly obvious that authors derive their works. That the drama must needs be closely related to the dramatist is just one of those simple discoveries that invariably elude the subtle professional mind; but in this wiser hour I may be permitted to assume that the author was the conscious father of his novel, and that he did not find it surprisingly in his pocket one morning, like a bad shilling taken in change from the cabman overnight.

Before he published his novel at the ripe age of thirty-seven the author had lived an irreproachable and gentlemanly life. Born with at least a German-silver spoon in his mouth, he passed, after a normally eventful childhood, through a respectable public school, and spent several agreeable years at Cambridge without taking a degree. He then went into his uncle's office in the City, where he idled daily from ten to four, till in due course he was admitted to a partnership, which enabled him to reduce his hours of idleness to eleven to three. These details become important when we reflect that from his childhood on the author had a great deal of time at his disposal. If he had been entirely normal, he would have accepted the conventions of the society to which he belonged, and devoted himself to motoring, bridge, and the encouragement of the lighter drama. But some deep-rooted habit of his childhood, or even perhaps some remote hereditary taint, led him to spend an appreciable fraction of his leisure time in the reading of works of fiction. Unlike most lovers of light literature, he read with a certain mental concentration, and was broad-minded enough to read good novels as well as bad ones.

It is a pleasant fact that it is impossible to concentrate one's mind on anything without in time becoming wiser, and in the course of years the author became quite a skilful critic of novels. From the first he had allowed his reading to colour his impressions of life, and had obediently lived in a world of blacks and whites, of heroes and heroines, of villains and adventuresses, until the grateful discovery of the realistic school of fiction permitted him to believe that men and women were for the most part neither good nor bad, but tabby. Moreover, the leisurely reading of many sentences had given him some understanding of the elements of style. He perceived that some combinations of words were illogical, and that others were unlovely to the ear ; and at the same time he acquired a vocabulary and a knowledge of grammar and punctuation that his earlier education had failed to give him. He read new novels at his writing-table, and took pleasure in correcting the mistakes of their authors in ink. When he had done this, he would hand them to his wife, who always read the end first, and, indeed, rarely pursued her investigation of a book beyond the last chapter.

We buy knowledge with illusions, and pay a high price for it, for the acquirement of quite a small degree of wisdom will deprive us of a large number of pleasant fancies. So it was with the author, who found his joy in novel-reading diminishing rapidly as his critical knowledge increased. He was no longer able to lose himself between the covers of a romance, but slid his paper-knife between the pages of a book with an unwholesome readiness to be irritated by the ignorance and folly of the novelist. His destructive criticism of works of fiction became so acute that it was natural that his unlettered friends should suggest that he himself ought to write a novel. For a long while he was content to receive the flattering suggestion with a reticent smile that masked his conviction that there was a difference between criticism and creation. But as he grew older the imperfections in the books he read ceased to give him the thrill of the successful explorer in sight of the expected, and time began to trickle too slowly through his idle fingers. One day he sat down and wrote " Chapter I. " at the head of a sheet of quarto paper.

It seemed to him that the difficulty was only one of selection, and he wrote two-thirds of a novel with a breathless ease of creation that made him marvel at himself and the pitiful struggles of less gifted novelists. Then in a moment of insight he picked up his manuscript and realised that what he had written was childishly crude. He had felt his story while he wrote it, but somehow or other he had failed to get his emotions on paper, and he saw quite clearly that it was worse and not better than the majority of the books which he had held up to ridicule.

There was a certain doggedness in his character that might have made him a useful citizen but for that unfortunate hereditary

spoon, and he wrote "Chapter I." at the head
of a new sheet of quarto paper long before the
library fire had reached the heart of his first
luckless manuscript. This time he wrote
more slowly, and with a waning confidence
that failed him altogether when he was about
half-way through. Reading the fragment
dispassionately he thought there were good
pages in it, but, taken as a whole, it was unequal, and moved forward only by fits and
starts. He began again with his late manuscript spread about him on the table for
reference. At the fifth attempt he succeeded
in writing a whole novel.

In the course of his struggles he had acquired a philosophy of composition. Especially he had learned to shun those
enchanted hours when the labour of creation
became suspiciously easy, for he had found by
experience that the work he did in these
moments of inspiration was either bad in itself
or out of key with the preceding chapters.
He thought that inspiration might be useful
to poets or writers of short stories, but
personally as a novelist he found it a nuisance.
By dint of hard work, however, he succeeded

in eliminating its evil influence from his final draft. He told himself that he had no illusions as to the merits of his book. He knew he was not a man of genius, but he knew also that the grammar and the punctuation of his novel were far above the average of such works, and although he could not read Sir Thomas Browne or Walter Pater with pleasure, he felt sure that his book was written in a straightforward and gentlemanly style. He was prepared to be told that his use of the colon was audacious, and looked forward with pleasure to an agreeable controversy on the question.

He read his book to his friends, who made suggestions that would have involved its re-writing from one end to the other. He read it to his enemies, who told him that it was nearly good enough to publish ; he read it to his wife, who said that it was very nice, and that it was time to dress for dinner. No one seemed to realise that it was the most important thing he had ever done in his life. This quickened his eagerness to get it published—an eagerness only tempered by a very real fear of those knowing dogs, the critics. He could not forget that he had criticised a good many books himself in terms that would have made the authors abandon their profession if they had but heard his strictures; and he had read notices in the papers that would have made him droop with shame if they had referred to any work of his. When these sombre thoughts came to him he would pick up his book and read it again, and in common fairness he had to admit to himself that he found it uncommonly good.

One day, after a whole batch of ungrammatical novels had reached him from the library, he posted his manuscript to his favourite publisher. He had heard stories of masterpieces many times rejected, so he did not tell his wife what he had done.

II. THE SLEEPY PUBLISHER

The publisher to whom our author had confided his manuscript stood, like all publishers, at the very head of his profession. His business was conducted on sound conservative lines, which means that though he had regretfully abandoned the three-volume

novel for the novel published at six shillings,
he was not among the intrepid revolutionaries
who were beginning to produce new fiction
at a still lower price. Besides novels he
published solid works of biography at thirty-
one and six, art books at a guinea, travel
books at fifteen shillings, flighty historical
works at twelve-and-sixpence, and cheap
editions of Montaigne's Essays and " Robinson
Crusoe " at a shilling. Some idea of his
business methods may be derived from the
fact that it pleased him to reflect that all
the other publishers were producing exactly
the same books as he was. And though he
would admit that the trade had been ruined
by competition and the outrageous royalties
demanded by successful authors, and, further,
that he made a loss on every separate depart-
ment of his business, in some mysterious
fashion the business as a whole continued
to pay him very well. He left the active
part of the management to a confidential
clerk, and contented himself with signing
cheques and interviewing authors.

With such a publisher the fate of our
author's book was never in doubt. If it was

lacking in those qualities that might be expected to commend it to the reading public, it was conspicuously rich in those merits that determine the favourable judgment of publishers' readers. It was above all things a gentlemanly book, without violence and without eccentricities. It was carefully and grammatically written; but it had not that exotic literary flavour which is so tiresome on a long railway journey. It could be put into the hands of any schoolgirl, and at most would merely send her to sleep. The only thing that could be said against it was that the author's dread of inspiration had made it grievously dull, but it was the publisher's opinion that after a glut of sensational fiction the six-shilling public had come to regard dullness as the hall-mark of literary merit. He had no illusions as to its possible success, but, on the other hand, he knew that he could not lose any money on it, so he wrote a letter to the author inviting him to an interview.

As soon as he had read the letter the author told himself that he had been certain all along that his book would be accepted. Nevertheless, he went to the interview moved by certain emotional flutterings against which circumstance had guarded him ever since his boyhood. He found this mild excitation of the nervous system by no means unpleasant. It was like digesting a new and subtle liqueur that made him light-footed and tingled in the tips of his fingers. He recalled a phrase that had greatly pleased him in the early days of his novel. " As the sun colours flowers, so Art colours life." It seemed to him that this was beginning to come true, and that life was already presenting itself to him in a gayer, brighter dress. He reached the publisher's office, therefore, in an unwontedly receptive mood, and was tremendously impressed by the rudeness of the clerks, who treated authors as mendicants and expressed their opinion of literature by handling books as if they were bundles of firewood.

The publisher looked at him under heavy eyelids, recognised his position in the social scale, and reflected with satisfaction that his acquaintances could be relied on to purchase at least a hundred copies. The interview did not at all take the lines that the author in his innocence had expected, and in a surprisingly short space of time he found himself bowed out, with the duplicate of a contract in the pocket of his overcoat. In the outer office the confidential clerk took him in hand and led him to the door of an enormous cellar, lit by electricity and filled from one end to the other with bales and heaps of books. "Books!" said the confidential clerk, with the smile of a gamekeeper displaying his hand-reared pheasants. "There are a great many," the author said timidly. "Of course, we do not keep our stock here," the clerk explained. "These are just samples." It was sometimes necessary to remind inexperienced writers that the publication of their first book was only a trivial incident in the history of a great publishing house. The author had a sad vision of his novel as a little brick in a monstrous pyramid built of books, and the clerk mentally decided that he was not the kind of man to turn up every day at the office to ask them how they were getting on.

The author was a little dazed when he

emerged into the street and the sunshine. His book, which an hour before had seemed the most important thing in the world, had become almost insignificant in the light of that vast collection of printed matter, and in some subtle way he felt that he had dwindled with it. The publisher had praised it without enthusiasm and had not specified any of its merits; he had not even commented on his fantastic use of the colon. The author had lived with it now for many months—it had become a part of his personality, and he felt that he had betrayed himself in delivering it into the hands of strangers who could not understand it. He had the reticence of the well-bred Englishman, and though he told himself reassuringly that his novel in no way reflected his private life, he could not quite overcome the sentiment that it was a little vulgar to allow alien eyes to read the product of his most intimate thoughts. He had really been shocked at the matter-of-fact way in which every one at the office had spoken of his book, and the sight of all the other books with which it would soon be inextricably confused had emphasised the

painful impression. This all seemed to rob
the author's calling of its presumed distinction,
and he looked at the men and women who
passed him on the pavement, and wondered
whether they too had written books.

This mood lasted for some weeks, at the end
of which time he received the proofs, which he
read and re-read with real pleasure before
setting himself to correcting them with
meticulous care. He performed this task
with such conscientiousness, and made so
many minor alterations—he changed most
of those flighty colons to more conventional
semicolons—that the confidential clerk swore
terribly when he glanced at the proofs before
handing them to a boy, with instructions to
remove three-quarters of the offending
emendations. A week or two later there
happened one of those strange little incidents
that make modern literary history. It was
a bright, sunny afternoon; the publisher
had been lunching with the star author of
the firm, a novelist whose books were read
wherever the British flag waved and there
was a circulating library to distribute them,
and now, in the warm twilight of the lowered

blinds he was enjoying profound thoughts, delicately tinted by burgundy and old port. The shrewdest men make mistakes, and certainly it was hardly wise of the confidential clerk to choose this peaceful moment to speak about our author's book. " I suppose we shall print a thousand?" he said. "Five thousand!" ejaculated the publisher. What was he thinking about? Was he filling up an imaginary income-tax statement, or was he trying to estimate the number of butterflies that seemed to float in the amber shadows of the room? The clerk did not know. "I suppose you mean one thousand, sir?" he said gently. The publisher was now wide awake. He had lost all his butterflies, and he was not the man to allow himself to be sleepy in the afternoon. " I said five thousand!" The clerk bit his lip and left the room.

The author never heard of this brief dialogue ; probably if he had been present he would have missed its significance. He would never have connected it with the flood of paragraphs that appeared in the Press announcing that the acumen of the publisher had discovered a new author of genius—paragraphs wherein he was compared with Dickens, Thackeray, Flaubert, Richardson, Sir Walter Besant, Thomas Browne, and the author of " An Englishwoman's Love-letters." As it was, it did not occur to him to wonder why the publisher should spend so much money on advertising a book of which he had seemed to have but a half-hearted appreciation. After all it was his book, and the author felt that it was only natural that as the hour of publication drew near the world of letters should show signs of a dignified excitement.

III. THE CRITIC ERRANT

There are some emotions so intimate that the most intrepid writer hesitates to chronicle them lest it should be inferred that he himself is in the confessional. We have endeavoured to show our author as a level-headed Englishman with his nerves well under control and an honest contempt for emotionalism in the stronger sex; but his feelings in the face of the first little bundle of reviews sent him by the press-cutting agency would prove this portrait incomplete. He noticed with a vague astonishment that the flimsy scraps of paper were trembling in his fingers like banknotes in the hands of a gambler, and he laid them down on the breakfast-table in disgust of the feminine weakness. This unmistakable proof that he had written a book, a real book, made him at once happy and uneasy. These fragments of smudged prints were his passport into a new and delightful world; they were, it might be said, the name of his destination in the great republic of letters, and yet he hesitated to look at them. He heard of the curious blindness of authors that made it impossible for them to detect the most egregious failings in their own work, and it occurred to him that this might be his malady. Why had he published his book? He felt at that moment that he had taken too great a risk. It would have been so easy to have had it privately printed and contented himself with distributing it among his friends. But these people who were paid for writing about books, these critics who had sent Keats to his gallipots and Swinburne to his fig-tree, might well

have failed to have recognised that his book
was sacred, because it was his own.

When he had at last achieved a fatalistic
tranquillity, he once more picked up the
notices, and this time he read them through
carefully. The *Rutlandshire Gazette* quoted
Shakespeare, the *Thrums Times* compared
him with Christopher North, the *Stamford-
bridge Herald* thought that his style resembled
that of Macaulay, but they were unanimous
in praising his book without reservation. It
seemed to the author that he was listening
to the authentic voice of fame. He rested his
chin on his hand and dreamed long dreams.

He could afford in this hour of his triumph
to forget the annoyances he had undergone
since his book was first accepted. The publisher, with a large first edition to dispose of,
had been rather more than firm with the
author. He had changed the title of the book
from "Earth's Returns"—a title that had
seemed to the author dignified and pleasantly
literary—to "The Improbable Marquis," which
seemed to him to mean nothing at all. Moreover, instead of giving the book a quiet and
scholarly exterior, he had bound it in boards

of an injudicious heliotrope, inset with a nasty little coloured picture of a young woman with a St. Bernard dog. This binding revolted the author, who objected, with some reason, that in all his book there was no mention of a dog of that description, or, indeed, of any dog at all. The book was wrapped in an outer cover that bore a recommendation of its contents, starting with a hideous split infinitive and describing it as an exquisite social comedy written from within. On the whole it seemed to the author that his book was flying false and undesirable colours, and since art lies outside the domesticities, he was hardly relieved when his wife told him that she thought the binding was very pretty. The author had shuddered no less at the little paragraphs that the publisher had inserted in the newspapers concerning his birth and education, wherein he was bracketed with other well-known writers whose careers at the University had been equally undistinguished. But now that, like Byron, he found himself famous among the bacon and eggs, he was in no mood to remember these past vexations. As soon as he had finished breakfast he withdrew himself to his study and wrote half an essay on the Republic of Letters.

In a country wherein fifteen novels—or is it fifty ?—are published every day of the year, the publisher's account of the goods he sells is bound to have a certain value. Money talks, as Mr. Arnold Bennett once observed— indeed to-day it is grown quite garrulous— and when a publisher spends a lot of money on advertising a book, the inference is that some one believes the book to be good. This will not secure a book good notices, but it will secure it notices of some kind or other, and that, as every publisher knows, is three-quarters of the battle. The average critic to-day is an old young man who has not failed in literature or art, possibly because he has not tried to accomplish anything in either. By the time he has acquired some skill in criticism he has generally ceased to be a critic, through no fault of his own, but through sheer weariness of spirit. When a man is very young he can dance upon every one who has not written a masterpiece with a light heart, but after this period of joyous savagery there follows fatigue and a certain pity. The critic loses sight of his first magnificent standards, and becomes grateful for even the smallest merit in the books he is compelled to read. Like a mother giving a powder to her child, he is at pains to disguise his timid censure with a teaspoonful of jam. As the years pass by he becomes afraid of these books that continue to appear in unreasonable profusion, and that have long ago destroyed his faith in literature, his love of reading, his sense of humour, and the colouring matter of his hair. He realises, with a dreadful sense of the infinite, that when he is dead and buried this torrent of books will overwhelm the individualities of his successors, bound like himself to a lifelong examination of the insignificant.

Timidity is certainly the note of modern criticism, which is rarely roused to indignation save when confronted by the infrequent outrage of some intellectual anarchist. If the critics of the more important journals were not so enthusiastic as their provincial *confrères*, they were at least gentle with " The Improbable Marquis." A critic of genius would have said that such books were not worth writing, still less worth reading. An out-

spoken critic would have said that it was too
dull to be an acceptable presentation of a life
that we all find interesting. As it was, most
of the critics praised the style in which it was
written because it was quite impossible to call
it an enthralling or even an entertaining book.
Some of the younger critics, who still retained
an interest in their own personalities, discovered
that its vacuity made it a convenient mirror
by means of which they would display the
progress of their own genius. In common
gratitude they had to close these manifestations of their merit with a word or two in
praise of the book they were professing to
review. "The Improbable Marquis" was very
favourably received by the Press in general.

It was, as the publisher made haste to point
out in his advertisements, a book of the year,
and, reassured by its flippant exterior, the
libraries and the public bought it with avidity.
The author pasted his swollen collection of
newspaper-cuttings into an album, and carefully revised his novel in case a second edition
should be called for. There was one review
which he had read more often than any of the
others, and nevertheless he hesitated to include

it in his collection. "This book," wrote the anonymous reviewer, "is as nearly faultless as a book may be that possesses no positive merit. It differs only from seven-eighths of the novels that are produced to-day in being more carefully written. The author had nothing to say, and he has said it." That was all, three malignant lines in a paper of no commercial importance, the sort of thing that was passed round the publisher's office with an appreciative chuckle. In the face of the general amiability of the Press, such a notice in an obscure journal could do the book no harm.

Only the author sat hour after hour in his study with that diminutive scrap of paper before him on the table, and wondered if it was true.

IV. FAME

It was some little time before the public, the mysterious section of the public that reads works of fiction, discovered that the publisher, aided by the normal good-humour of the critics, had persuaded them to sacrifice some of their scant hours of intellectual recreation

on a work of portentous dullness. Then—
for the literary audience has its sense of
humour—they amused themselves for a while
by recommending the book to their friends,
and the sales crept steadily up to four
thousand, and there stayed with an unmistakable air of finality. If the book had had
any real literary merit its life would have
started at that point, for the weary comments
of reviewers and the strident outcries of publishers tend to obscure rather than reveal
the permanent value of a book. But six
months after publication " The Improbable
Marquis " was completely forgotten, save by
the second-hand booksellers, who found themselves embarrassed with a number of books
for which no one seemed anxious to pay six-
pence, in spite of the striking heliotrope
binding. The publisher, who was aware of
this circumstance, offered the author five
hundred copies at cost price, and the author
bought them, and sent them to public
libraries, without examining the motive for
his action too closely. There were moments
when he regarded the success of his book
with suspicion. He would have preferred

the praise that had greeted it to have been less violent and more clearly defined. Of all the criticisms, the only one that lingered in his mind was the curt comment, "The author had nothing to say, and he has said it." He thought it was unfair, but he had remembered it. At the same time, in examining his own character, he could not find that masterfulness that seemed to him necessary in a great man. But for the most part he was content to accept his new honours with a placid satisfaction, and to smile genially upon a world that was eager to credit him with qualities that possibly he did not possess.

For if his book was no longer read his fame as an author seemed to be established on a rock. Society, with a larger S than that which he had hitherto adorned, was delighted to find after two notable failures that genius could still be presentable, and the author was rather more than that. He was rich, he had that air of the distinguished army officer which falls so easily to those who occupy the pleasant position of sleeping partner in the City, and he had just the right shade of amused modesty with which to meet inquiries as to his literary intentions. In a word, he was an author of whom any country—even France, that prolific parent of presentable authors—would have been proud. Even his wife, who had thought it an excellent joke that her husband should have written a book, had to take him seriously as an author when she found that their social position was steadily improving. With feminine tact she gave him a fountain-pen on his birthday, from which he was meant to conclude that she believed in his mission as an artist.

Meanwhile, with the world at his feet, the author spent an appreciable part of his time in visiting the second-hand bookshops and buying copies of his book absurdly cheap. He carried these waifs home and stored them in an attic secretly, for he would have found it hard to explain his motives to the intellectually childless. In the first flush of authorship he had sent a number of presentation copies of his book to writers whom he admired, and he noticed without bitterness that some of these volumes with their neatly turned inscriptions were coming back to him through this channel. At all the second-hand bookshops he saw long-haired young men looking over the books without buying them, and he thought these must be authors, but he was too shy to speak to them, though he had a great longing to know other writers. He wanted to ask them questions concerning their methods of work, for he was having trouble with his second book. He had read an article in which the writer said that the great fault of modern fiction was that authors were more concerned to produce good chapters than to produce good books. It seemed to him that in his first book he had only aimed at good sentences, but he knew no one with whom he could discuss such matters.

One day he found a copy of "The Improbable Marquis" in the Charing Cross Road, and was glancing through it with absent-minded interest, when a voice at his elbow said, "I shouldn't buy that if I were you, sir. It's no good!" He looked up and saw a wild young man, with bright eyes and an untidy black beard. "But it's mine; I wrote it," cried the author. The young

man stared at him in dismay. "I'm sorry ;
I didn't know," he blurted out, and faded
away into the crowd. The author gazed
after him wistfully, regretting that he had
not had presence of mind enough to ask
him to lunch. Perhaps the young man could
have told him how he ought to write his
second book.

For somehow or other, at the very moment
when his literary position seemed most secure
in the eyes of his wife and his friends, the
author had lost all confidence in his own
powers. He shut himself up in his study every
night, and was supposed by an admiring and
almost timorous household to be producing
masterpieces, when in reality he was conduct-
ing a series of barren skirmishes between the
critical and the creative elements of his nature.
He would write a chapter or two in a fine
fury of composition, and then would read
what he had written with intense disgust.
He felt that his second book ought to be
better than his first, and he doubted whether
he would even be able to write anything half
so good. In his hour of disillusionment he
recalled the anonymous critic who had treated

"The Improbable Marquis" with such scant respect, and he wrote to him asking him to expand his judgment. He was prepared to be wounded by the answer, but the form it took surprised him. In reply to his temperate and courteous letter the critic sent a postcard bearing only five short words— "Why did you write it?"

This was bad manners, but the author was sensible enough to see that it might be good criticism, especially as he found some difficulty in answering the question. Why had he written a book? Not for money, or for fame, or to express a personality of which he saw no reason to be proud. All his friends had said that he ought to write a novel, and he had thought that he could write a better one than the average. But he had to admit that such motives seemed to him insufficient. There was, perhaps, some mysterious force that drove men to create works of art, and the critic had seen that his book had lacked this necessary impulse. In the light of this new theory the author was roused by a sense of injustice. He felt that it should be possible for any one to write a good book

if they took sufficient pains, and he set himself to work again with a savage and unpro-
ductive energy.

It seemed to him that in spite of his effort
to bear in mind that the whole should be
greater than any part, his chapters broke up
into sentences and his sentences into forlorn
and ungregarious words. When he looked
to his first book for comfort he found the
same horrid phenomenon taking place in its
familiar pages. Sometimes when he was dis-
heartened by his fruitless efforts he slipped
out into the streets, fixing his attention on
concrete objects to rest his tired mind. But
he could not help noticing that London had
discovered the secret which made his intellectual life a torment. The streets were
more than a mere assemblage of houses,
London herself was more than a tangled
skein of streets, and overhead heaven was
more than a meeting-place of individual stars.
What was this secret that made words into
a book, houses into cities, and restless and
measurable stars into an unchanging and
immeasurable universe ?

THE BIRD IN THE GARDEN

THE room in which the Burchell family lived in Love Street, S.E., was underground and depended for light and air on a grating let into the pavement above.

Uncle John, who was a queer one, had filled the area with green plants and creepers in boxes and tins hanging from the grating, so that the room itself obtained very little light indeed, but there was always a nice bright green place for the people sitting in it to look at. Toby, who had peeped into the areas of other little boys, knew that his was of quite exceptional beauty, and it was with a certain awe that he helped Uncle John to tend the plants in the morning, watering them and taking the pieces of paper and straws that had fallen through the grating from their hair. " It is a great mistake to have straws in one's hair," Uncle John would say gravely; and Toby knew that it was true.

It was in the morning after they had just been watered that the plants looked and smelt best, and when the sun shone through the grating and the diamonds were shining and falling through the forest, Toby would tell the baby about the great bird who would one day come flying through the trees—a bird of all colours, ugly and beautiful, with a harsh sweet voice. "And that will be the end of everything," said Toby, though of course he was only repeating a story his Uncle John had told him.

There were other people in the big, dark room besides Toby and Uncle John and the baby ; dark people who flitted to and fro about secret matters, people called father and mother and Mr. Hearn, who were apt to kick if they found you in their way, and who never laughed except at nights, and then they laughed too loudly.

"They will frighten the bird," thought Toby; but they were kind to Uncle John because he had a pension. Toby slept in a corner on the ground beside the baby, and

when father and Mr. Hearn fought at nights
he would wake up and watch and shiver; but
when this happened it seemed to him that
the baby was laughing at him, and he would
pinch her to make her stop. One night, when
the men were fighting very fiercely and mother
had fallen asleep on the table, Uncle John rose
from his bed and began singing in a great
voice. It was a song Toby knew very well
about Trafalgar's Bay, but it frightened the
two men a great deal because they thought
Uncle John would be too mad to fetch the
pension any more. Next day he was quite
well, however, and he and Toby found a large
green caterpillar in the garden among the
plants.

"This is a fact of great importance," said
Uncle John, stroking it with a little stick.
"It is a sign!"

Toby used to lie awake at nights after that
and listen for the bird, but he only heard the
clatter of feet on the pavement and the
screaming of engines far away.

Later there came a new young woman to
live in the cellar—not a dark person, but a
person you could see and speak to. She patted

Toby on the head; but when she saw the baby she caught it to her breast and cried over it, calling it pretty names.

At first father and Mr. Hearn were both very kind to her, and mother used to sit all day in the corner with burning eyes, but after a time the three used to laugh together at -nights as before, and the woman would sit with her wet face and wait for the coming of the bird, with Toby and the baby and Uncle John, who was a queer one.

"All we have to do," Uncle John would say, "is to keep the garden clean and tidy, and to water the plants every morning so that they may be very green." And Toby would go and whisper this to the baby, and she would stare at the ceiling with large, stupid eyes.

There came a time when Toby was very sick, and he lay all day in his corner wondering about wonder. Sometimes the room in which he lay became so small that he was choked for lack of air, sometimes it was so large that he screamed out because he felt lonely. He could not see the dark people then at all, but only Uncle John and the woman, who told him in whispers that her

name was " Mummie." She called him Sonny,
which is a very pretty name, and when Toby
heard it he felt a tickling in his sides which he
knew to be gladness. Mummie's face was wet
and warm and soft, and she was very fond of
kissing. Every morning Uncle John would
lift Toby up and show him the garden, and
Toby would slip out of his arms and walk
among the trees and plants. And the place
would grow bigger and bigger until it was all
the world, and Toby would lose himself
amongst the tangle of trees and flowers and
creepers. He would see butterflies there and
tame animals, and the sky was full of birds of
all colours, ugly and beautiful; but he knew
that none of these was the bird, because their
voices were only sweet. Sometimes he showed
these wonders to a little boy called Toby, who
held his hand and called him Uncle John,
sometimes he showed them to his mummie
and he himself was Toby; but always when he
came back he found himself lying in Uncle
John's arms, and, weary from his walk, would
fall into a pleasant dreamless sleep.
    It seemed to Toby at this time that a veil
hung about him which, dim and unreal in

itself, served to make all things dim and
unreal. He did not know whether he was
asleep or awake, so strange was life, so vivid
were his dreams. Mummie, Uncle John, the
baby, Toby himself came with a flicker of the
veil and disappeared vaguely without cause.
It would happen that Toby would be speaking
to Uncle John, and suddenly he would find
himself looking into the large eyes of the baby,
turned stupidly towards the ceiling, and again
the baby would be Toby himself, a hot, dry
little body without legs or arms, that swayed
suspended as if by magic a foot above the
bed.

Then there was the vision of two small feet
that moved a long way off, and Toby would
watch them curiously as kittens do their tails,
without knowing the cause of their motion.

It was all very wonderful and very strange,
and day by day the veil grew thicker; there
was no need to wake when the sleeptime was
so pleasant; there were no dark people to kick
you in that dreamy place.

And yet Toby woke—woke to a life and in
a place which he had never known before.

He found himself on a heap of rags in a

large cellar which depended for its light on a grating let into the pavement of the street above. On the stone floor of the area and swinging from the grating were a few sickly, grimy plants in pots. There must have been a fine sunset up above, for a faint red glow came through the bars and touched the leaves of the plants.

There was a lighted candle standing in a bottle on the table, and the cellar seemed full of people. At the table itself two men and a woman were drinking, though they were already drunk, and beyond in a corner Toby could see the head and shoulders of a tall old man. Beside him there crouched a woman with a faded, pretty face, and between Toby and the rest of the room there stood a box in which lay a baby with large, wakeful eyes.

Toby's body tingled with excitement, for this was a new thing; he had never seen it before, he had never seen anything before.

The voice of the woman at the table rose and fell steadily without a pause; she was abusing the other woman, and the two drunken men were laughing at her and shouting her on; Toby thought the other woman lacked spirit because she stayed crouching on the floor and said nothing.

At last the woman stopped her abuse, and one of the men turned and shouted an order to the woman on the floor. She stood up and came towards him, hesitating; this annoyed the man and he swore at her brutally; when she came near enough he knocked her down with his fist, and all the three burst out laughing.

Toby was so excited that he knelt up in his corner and clapped his hands, but the others did not notice because the old man was up and swaying wildly over the woman. He seemed to be threatening the man who had struck her, and that one was evidently afraid of him, for he rose unsteadily and lifted the chair on which he had been sitting above his head to use as a weapon.

The old man raised his fist and the chair fell heavily on to his wrinkled forehead and he dropped to the ground.

The woman at the table cried out, "The pension!" in her shrill voice, and then they were all quiet, looking.

Then it seemed to Toby that through the forest there came flying, with a harsh sweet voice and a tumult of wings, a bird of all colours, ugly and beautiful, and he knew, though later there might be people to tell him otherwise, that that was the end of everything.

CHILDREN OF THE MOON

THE boy stood at the place where the park trees stopped and the smooth lawns slid away gently to the great house. He was dressed only in a pair of ragged knickerbockers and a gaping buttonless shirt, so that his legs and neck and chest shone silver bare in the moonlight. By day he had a mass of rough golden hair, but now it seemed to brood above his head like a black cloud that made his face deathly white by comparison. On his arms there lay a great heap of gleaming dew-wet roses and lilies, spoil of the park flower-beds. Their cool petals touched his cheek, and filled his nostrils with aching scent. He felt his arms smarting here and there, where the thorns of the roses had torn them in the dark, but these delicate caresses of pain only served to deepen to him the wonder of the night that wrapped him about like a cloak. Behind him there dreamed the black woods, and over his head multitudinous stars quivered and balanced in space; but these things were nothing to him, for far across the lawn that was spread knee-deep with a web of mist there gleamed for his eager eyes the splendour of a fairy palace. Red and orange and gold, the lights of the fairy revels shone from a hundred windows and filled him with wonder that he should see with wakeful eyes the jewels that he had desired so long in sleep. He could only gaze and gaze until his straining eyes filled with tears, and set the enchanted lights dancing in the dark. On his ears, that heard no more the crying of the night-birds and the quick stir of the rabbits in the brake, there fell the strains of far music. The flowers in his arms seemed to sway to it, and his heart beat to the deep pulse of the night.

So enraptured were his senses that he did not notice the coming of the girl, and she was able to examine him closely before she called to him softly through the moonlight.

"Boy! Boy!"

At the sound of her voice he swung round and looked at her with startled eyes.

He saw her excited little face and her white dress.

"Are you a fairy?" he asked hoarsely, for the night-mist was in his voice.

"No," she said, "I'm a little girl. You're a wood-boy, I suppose?"

He stayed silent, regarding her with a puzzled face. Who was this little white creature with the tender voice that had slipped so suddenly out of the night?

"As a matter of fact," the girl continued, I've come out to have a look at the fairies. There's a ring down in the wood. You can come with me if you like, wood-boy."

He nodded his head silently, for he was afraid to speak to her, and set off through the wood by her side, still clasping the flowers to his breast.

"What were you looking at when I found you?" she asked.

"The palace—the fairy palace," the boy muttered.

"The palace?" the girl repeated. "Why, that's not a palace; that's where I live."

The boy looked at her with new awe; if she were a fairy—— But the girl had noticed that his feet made no sound beside her shoes.

" Don't the thorns prick your feet, wood-boy ? " she asked; but the boy said nothing, and they were both silent for a while, the girl looking about her keenly as she walked, and the boy watching her face. Presently they came to a wide pool where a little tinkling fountain threw bubbles to the hidden fish.

" Can you swim ? " she said to the boy.

He shook his head.

" It's a pity," said the girl; " we might have had a bathe.   It would be rather fun in the dark, but it's pretty deep there.   We'd better get on to the fairy ring."

The moon had flung queer shadows across the glade in which the ring lay, and when they stood on the edge listening intently the wood seemed to speak to them with a hundred voices.

" You can take hold of my hand, if you like," said the girl, in a whisper.

The boy dropped his flowers about his white feet and felt for the girl's hand in the dark. Soon it lay in his own, a warm live thing, that stirred a little with excitement

" I'm not afraid," the girl said; and so they waited.

The man came upon them suddenly from among the silver birches. He had a knapsack on his back and his hair was as long as a tramp's. At sight of him the girl almost screamed, and her hand trembled in the boy's; some instinct made him hold it tighter.

" What do you want ? " he muttered, in his hoarse voice.

The man was no less astonished than the children.

" What on earth are you doing here ? " he cried. His voice was mild and reassuring, and the girl answered him promptly.

" I came out to look for fairies."

" Oh, that's right enough," commented the man; " and you," he said, turning to the boy, " are you after fairies, too ? Oh, I see; picking flowers. Do you mean to sell them ? "

The boy shook his head.

" For my sister," he said, and stopped abruptly.

" Is your sister fond of flowers ? "

" Yes; she's dead."

The man looked at him gravely.

" That's a phrase," he said, " and phrases are the devil. Who told you that dead people like flowers ? "

" They always have them," said the boy, blushing for shame of his pretty thought.

" And what are *you* looking for ? " the girl interrupted.

The man made a mocking grimace, and glanced around the glade as if he were afraid of being overheard.

" Dreams," he said bluntly.

The girl pondered this for a moment.

" And your knapsack ? " she began.

" Yes," said the man, " it's full of them."

The children looked at the knapsack with interest, the girl's fingers tingling to undo the straps of it.

" What are they like ? " she asked.

The man gave a short laugh.

" Very like yours and his, I expect; when you grow older, young woman, you'll find there's really only one dream possible for a sensible person. But you don't want to hear about my troubles. This is more in your line." He put his hand in his pocket and

pulled out a flageolet, which he put to his lips.
" Listen ! " he said.

To the girl it seemed as though the little
tune had leapt from the pipe, and was dancing
round the ring like a real fairy, while echo
came tripping through the trees to join it.
The boy gaped and said nothing.

At last, when the fairy was beginning to
falter and echo was quite out of breath, the
man took the flageolet from his lips.

" Well," he said, with a smile.

" Thank you very much," said the girl
politely. " I think that was very nice indeed.
Oh, boy ! " she broke off, " you're hurting my
hand ! "

The boy's eyes were shining strangely, and
he was waving his arms in dismay.

" All the wasted moonlight ! " he cried ;
the grass is quite wet with it."

The girl turned to him in surprise.

" Why, boy, you've found your voice."

" After that," said the man gravely,
as he put his flageolet back in his pocket,
" I think I will show you the inside of my
knapsack."

The girl bent down eagerly, while he

loosened the straps, but gave a cry of disappointment when she saw the contents.

" Pictures ! " she said.

" Pictures," echoed the man drily,—" pictures of dreams. I don't know how you're going to see them. Perhaps the moon will do her best."

The girl looked at them nicely, and passed them on one by one to the boy. Presently she made a discovery.

" Oh, boy ! " she cried, " your tears are spoiling all the pictures."

" I'm sorry," said the boy huskily ; " I can't help it."

" I know," the man said quickly ; " it doesn't matter a bit. I expect you've seen these pictures before."

" I know them all," said the boy, " but I have never seen them."

The man frowned.

" It's the devil," he said to himself, " when boys speak English." He turned suddenly to the girl, who was puzzling over the boy's tears. " It's time you went back to bed," he said ; " there won't be any fairies to-night. It's too cold for them."

The girl yawned.

"I shall get into a row when I get back if they've found it out. I don't care."

"The moon is fading," said the boy suddenly; "there are no more shadows."

"We will see you through the wood," the man continued, "and say good-night."

He put his pictures back in his knapsack and then walked silently through the murmuring wood. At the edge of the wood the girl stopped.

"You are a wood-boy," she said to the boy, "and you mustn't come any farther. You can give me a kiss if you like."

The boy did not move, but stayed regarding her awkwardly.

"I think you are a very silly boy," said the girl, with a toss of her head, and she stalked away proudly into the mist.

"Why didn't you kiss her?" asked the man.

"Her lips would burn me," said the boy.

The man and the boy walked slowly across the park.

"Now, boy," said the man, "since civilisation has gone to bed the time has come for you to hear your destiny."

"I am only a poor boy," the boy replied simply. "I don't think I have any destiny."

"Paradox," said the man, "is meant to conceal the insincerity of the aged, not to express the simplicity of youth. But I wander. You have made phrases to-night."

"What are phrases?"

"What are dreams? What are roses? What, in fine, is the moon? Boy, I take you for a moon-child. You hold her pale flowers in your arms, her white beams have caressed your limbs, you prefer the kisses of her cool lips to those of that earth-child; all this is very well. But, above all, you have the music of her great silence; above all, you have her tears. When I played to you on my pipe you recognised the voice of your mother. When I showed you my pictures you recalled the tales with which she hushed you to sleep. And so I knew that you were her son and my little brother."

"The moon has always been my friend," said the boy; "but I did not know that she was my mother."

"Perhaps your sister knows it; the happy dead are glad to seek her for a mother;

that is why they are so fond of white flowers."

"We have a mother at home. She works very hard for us."

"But it is your mother among the clouds who makes your life beautiful, and the beauty of your life is the measure of your days."

While the boy reflected on these things they had reached the gates of the park, and they stole past the silent lodge on to the high road. A man was waiting there in the shadows, and when he saw the boy's companion he rushed out and seized him by the arm.

"So I've got you," he said; "I don't think I'll let you go again in a hurry."

The son of the moon gave a queer little laugh.

"Why, it's Taylor!" he said pleasantly; "but, Taylor, you know you're making a great mistake."

"Very possibly," said the keeper, with a laugh.

"You see this boy here, Taylor; I assure you he is much madder than I am."

Taylor looked at the boy kindly.

"Time you were in bed, Tommy," he said.

"Taylor," said the man earnestly, "this boy has made three phrases. " If you don't lock him up he will certainly become a poet. He will set your precious world of sanity ablaze with the fire of his mother, the moon. Your palaces will totter, Taylor, and your kingdoms become as dust. I have warned you."

" That's right, sir; and now you must come with me."

"Boy," said the man generously, "keep your liberty. By grace of Providence, all men in authority are fools. We shall meet again under the light of the moon."

With dreamy eyes the boy watched the departure of his companion. He had become almost invisible along the road when, miraculously as it seemed, the light of the moon broke through the trees by the wayside and lit up his figure. For a moment it fell upon his head like a halo, and touched the knapsack of dreams with glory. Then all was lost in the blackness of night.

As he turned homeward the boy felt a cold wind upon his cheek. It was the first breath of dawn.

THE COFFIN MERCHANT

LONDON on a November Sunday inspired
Eustace Reynolds with a melancholy too
insistent to be ignored and too causeless to be
enjoyed. The grey sky overhead between the
house-tops, the cold wind round every street-
corner, the sad faces of the men and women
on the pavements, combined to create an
atmosphere of ineloquent misery. Eustace
was sensitive to impressions, and in spite of a
half-conscious effort to remain a dispassionate
spectator of the world's melancholy, he felt
the chill of the aimless day creeping over his
spirit. Why was there no sun, no warmth, no
laughter on the earth ? What had become of
all the children who keep laughter like a mask
on the faces of disillusioned men ? The wind
blew down Southampton Street, and chilled
Eustace to a shiver that passed away in a
shudder of disgust at the sombre colour of

life. A windy Sunday in London before the
lamps are lit, tempts a man to believe in the
nobility of work.

At the corner by Charing Cross Telegraph Office a man thrust a handbill under his
eyes, but he shook his head impatiently. The
blueness of the fingers that offered him the
paper was alone sufficient to make him dis-
inclined to remove his hands from his pockets
even for an instant. But the man would not
be dismissed so lightly.

"Excuse me, sir," he said, following him,
"you have not looked to see what my bills
are."

" Whatever they are I do not want them."

" That's where you are wrong, sir," the man
said earnestly. " You will never find life
interesting if you do not lie in wait for the
unexpected. As a matter of fact, I believe
that my bill contains exactly what you do
want."

Eustace looked at the man with quick
curiosity. His clothes were ragged, and the
visible parts of his flesh were blue with cold,
but his eyes were bright with intelligence and
his speech was that of an educated man. It

seemed to Eustace that he was being regarded
with a keen expectancy, as though his decision
on the trivial point was of real importance.

" I don't know what you are driving at,"
he said, " but if it will give you any pleasure
I will take one of your bills ; though if you
argue with all your clients as you have with
me, it must take you a long time to get rid
of them."

" I only offer them to suitable persons," the
man said, folding up one of the handbills
while he spoke, " and I'm sure you will not
regret taking it," and he slipped the paper into
Eustace's hand and walked rapidly away.

Eustace looked after him curiously for a
moment, and then opened the paper in his
hand. When his eyes comprehended its
significance, he gave a low whistle of astonishment. " You will soon be wanting a coffin ! "
it read. " At 606, Gray's Inn Road, your order
will be attended to with civility and despatch.
Call and see us ! ! "

Eustace swung round quickly to look for
the man, but he was out of sight. The wind
was growing colder, and the lamps were beginning to shine out in the greying streets.

Eustace crumpled the paper into his overcoat pocket, and turned homewards.

" How silly ! " he said to himself, in conscious amusement. The sound of his footsteps on the pavement rang like an echo to his laugh.

II

Eustace was impressionable but not temperamentally morbid, and he was troubled a little by the fact that the gruesomely bizarre handbill continued to recur to his mind. The thing was so manifestly absurd, he told himself with conviction, that it was not worth a second thought, but this did not prevent him from thinking of it again and again. What manner of undertaker could hope to obtain business by giving away foolish handbills in the street ? Really, the whole thing had the air of a brainless practical joke, yet his intellectual fairness forced him to admit that as far as the man who had given him the bill was concerned, brainlessness was out of the question, and joking improbable. There had been depths in those little bright

eyes which his glance had not been able to
sound, and the man's manner in making him
accept the handbill had given the whole
transaction a kind of ludicrous significance.

"You will soon be wanting a coffin——!"

Eustace found himself turning the words
over and over in his mind. If he had had any
near relations he might have construed the
thing as an elaborate threat, but he was prac-
tically alone in the world, and it seemed to
him that he was not likely to want a coffin
for any one but himself.

"Oh damn the thing!" he said impatiently, as he opened the door of his flat,
"it isn't worth worrying about. I mustn't
let the whim of some mad tradesman get
on my nerves. I've got no one to bury,
anyhow."

Nevertheless the thing lingered with him
all the evening, and when his neighbour the
doctor came in for a chat at ten o'clock,
Eustace was glad to show him the strange
handbill. The doctor, who had experienced
the queer magics that are practised to this
day on the West Coast of Africa, and who,
therefore, had no nerves, was delighted with

so striking an example of British commercial enterprise.

"Though, mind you," he added gravely, smoothing the crumpled paper on his knee, "this sort of thing might do a lot of harm if it fell into the hands of a nervous subject. I should be inclined to punch the head of the ass who perpetrated it. Have you turned that address up in the Post Office Directory?"

Eustace shook his head, and rose and fetched the fat red book which makes London an English city. Together they found the Gray's Inn Road, and ran their eyes down to No. 606.

"'Harding, G. J., Coffin Merchant and Undertaker.' Not much information there," muttered the doctor.

"Coffin merchant's a bit unusual, isn't it?" queried Eustace.

"I suppose he manufactures coffins wholesale for the trade. Still, I didn't know they called themselves that. Anyhow, it seems as though that handbill is a genuine piece of downright foolishness. The idiot ought to be stopped advertising in that way."

"I'll go and see him myself to-morrow," said Eustace bluntly.

"Well, he's given you an invitation," said the doctor, "so it's only polite of you to go. I'll drop in here in the evening to hear what he's like. I expect that you'll find him as mad as a hatter."

"Something like that," said Eustace, "or he wouldn't give handbills to people like me. I have no one to bury except myself."

"No," said the doctor in the hall, "I suppose you haven't. Don't let him measure you for a coffin, Reynolds!"

Eustace laughed.

"We never know," he said sententiously.

III

Next day was one of those gorgeous blue days of which November gives but few, and Eustace was glad to run out to Wimbledon for a game of golf, or rather for two. It was therefore dusk before he made his way to the Gray's Inn Road in search of the unexpected. His attitude towards his errand despite the doctor's laughter and the prosaic entry in the directory, was a little confused. He could not help reflecting that after all the doctor had not seen the man with the little wise eyes, nor could he forget that Mr. G. J. Harding's description of himself as a coffin merchant, to say the least of it, approached the unusual. Yet he felt that it would be intolerable to chop the whole business without finding out what it all meant. On the whole he would have preferred not to have discovered the riddle at all; but having found it, he could not rest without an answer.

No. 606, Gray's Inn Road, was not like an ordinary undertaker's shop. The window was heavily draped with black cloth, but was otherwise unadorned. There were no letters from grateful mourners, no little model coffins, no photographs of marble memorials. Even more surprising was the absence of any name over the shop-door, so that the uninformed stranger could not possibly tell what trade was carried on within, or who was responsible for the management of the business. This uncommercial modesty did not tend to remove Eustace's doubts as to the

sanity of Mr. G. J. Harding; but he opened
the shop-door which started a large bell
swinging noisily, and stepped over the thres-
hold. The shop was hardly more expressive
inside than out. A broad counter ran across
it, cutting it in two, and in the partial gloom
overhead a naked gas-burner whistled a noisy
song. Beyond this the shop contained no
furniture whatever, and no stock - in - trade
except a few planks leaning against the wall
in one corner. There was a large ink-stand
on the counter. Eustace waited patiently
for a minute or two, and then as no one
came he began stamping on the floor with
his foot. This proved efficacious, for soon
he heard the sound of footsteps ascending
wooden stairs, the door behind the counter
opened and a man came into the shop.

He was dressed quite neatly now, and his
hands were no longer blue with cold, but
Eustace knew at once that it was the man
who had given him the handbill. Nevertheless he looked at Eustace without a sign
of recognition.

" What can I do for you, sir ? " he asked
pleasantly.

Eustace laid the handbill down on the counter.

"I want to know about this," he said. "It strikes me as being in pretty bad taste, and if a nervous person got hold of it, it might be dangerous."

"You think so, sir? Yet our representative," he lingered affectionately on the words, "our representative told you, I believe, that the handbill was only distributed to suitable cases."

"That's where you are wrong," said Eustace sharply, "for I have no one to bury."

"Except yourself," said the coffin merchant suavely.

Eustace looked at him keenly. "I don't see——" he began. But the coffin merchant interrupted him.

"You must know, sir," he said, "that this is no ordinary undertaker's business. We possess information that enables us to defy competition in our special class of trade."

"Information!"

"Well, if you prefer it, you may say intuitions. If our representative handed you that advertisement, it was because he knew you would need it."

"Excuse me," said Eustace, "you appear to be sane, but your words do not convey to me any reasonable significance. You gave me that foolish advertisement yourself, and now you say that you did so because you knew I would need it. I ask you why ? "

The coffin merchant shrugged his shoulders. " Ours is a sentimental trade," he said, " I do not know why dead men want coffins, but they do. For my part I would wish to be cremated."

" Dead men ? "

" Ah, I was coming to that. You see Mr.—— ? "

" Reynolds."

" Thank you, my name is Harding—G. J. Harding. You see, Mr. Reynolds, our in-tuitions are of a very special character, and if we say that you will need a coffin, it is— probable that you will need one."

" You mean to say that I—— "

" Precisely. In twenty-four hours or less, Mr. Reynolds, you will need our services."

The revelation of the coffin merchant's in-

sanity came to Eustace with a certain relief.
For the first time in the interview he had a
sense of the dark empty shop and the
whistling gas-jet over his head.

"Why, it sounds like a threat, Mr.
Harding!" he said gaily.

The coffin merchant looked at him oddly,
and produced a printed form from his
pocket. "If you would fill this up," he
said.

Eustace picked it up off the counter and
laughed aloud. It was an order for a
hundred-guinea funeral.

"I don't know what your game is," he
said, "but this has gone on long enough."

"Perhaps it has, Mr. Reynolds," said the
coffin merchant, and he leant across the
counter and looked Eustace straight in the
face.

For a moment Eustace was amused; then
he was suddenly afraid. "I think it's time
I——" he began slowly, and then he was
silent, his whole will intent on fighting the
eyes of the coffin merchant. The song of
the gas-jet waned to a point in his ears, and
then rose steadily till it was like the beating

of the world's heart.   The eyes of the
coffin merchant grew larger and larger, till
they blended in one great circle of fire.   Then
Eustace picked a pen off the counter and
filled in the form.

" Thank you very much, Mr. Reynolds,"
said the coffin merchant, shaking hands with
him politely.   "I can promise you every civility
and despatch.   Good-day, sir."

Outside on the pavement Eustace stood for
a while trying to recall exactly what had
happened.   There was a slight scratch on his
hand, and when he automatically touched it
with his lips, it made them burn.   The lit
lamps in the Gray's Inn Road seemed to him
a little unsteady, and the passers-by showed a
disposition to blunder into him.

" Queer business," he said to himself dimly ;
" I'd better have a cab."

He reached home in a dream.

It was nearly ten o'clock before the doctor
remembered his promise, and went upstairs to
Eustace's flat.   The outer door was half-open
so that he thought he was expected, and he
switched on the light in the little hall, and
shut the door behind him with the simplicity

of habit.   But when he swung round from the door he gave a cry of astonishment.   Eustace was lying asleep in a chair before him with his face flushed and drooping on his shoulder, and his breath hissing noisily through his parted lips.   The doctor looked at him quizzically, " If 1 did not know you, my young friend," he remarked, " I should say that you were as drunk as a lord."

And he went up to Eustace and shook him by the shoulder ; but Eustace did not wake.

" Queer ! " the doctor muttered, sniffing at Eustace's lips ; " he hasn't been drinking."

THE SOUL OF A POLICEMAN

I

OUTSIDE, above the uneasy din of the traffic, the sky was glorious with the far peace of a fine summer evening. Through the upper pane of the station window Police-constable Bennett, who felt that his senses ' at the moment were abnormally keen, recognised with a sinking heart such reds and yellows as bedecked the best patchwork quilt at home. By contrast the lights of the superintendent's office were subdued, so that within the walls of the police-station sounds seemed of greater importance. Somewhere a drunkard, deprived of his boots, was drumming his criticism of authority on the walls of his cell. From the next room, where the men off duty were amusing themselves, there came a steady clicking of billiard-balls and dominoes, broken

now and again by gruff bursts of laughter.
And at his very elbow the superintendent was
speaking in that suave voice that reminded
Bennett of grey velvet.

"You see, Bennett, how matters stand.
I have nothing at all against your conduct.
You are steady and punctual, and I have
no doubt that you are trying to do your
duty.   But it's very unfortunate that as far
as results go you have nothing to show for
your efforts.   During the last three weeks
you have not brought in a charge of any
description, and during the same period I
find that your colleagues on the beat have
been exceptionally busy.   I repeat that I
do not accuse you of neglecting your duty,
but these things tell with the magistrates
and convey a general suggestion of slackness."

Bennett looked   down   at   his   brightly
polished boots.   His fingers were sandy and
there was soft felt beneath his feet.

"I have been afraid of this for some time,
sir," he said, "very much afraid."

The superintendent looked at him ques-
tioningly.

"You have nothing to say?" he said.

" I have always tried to do my duty, sir."

" I know, I know. But you must see that a certain number of charges, if not of convictions, is the mark of a smart officer."

" Surely you would not have me arrest innocent persons ? "

"That is a most improper observation," said the superintendent severely. " I will say no more to you now. But I hope you will take what I have said as a warning. You must bustle along, Bennett, bustle along."

Outside in the street, Police-constable Bennett was free to reflect on his unpleasant interview. The superintendent was ambitious and therefore pompous; he, himself, was unambitious and therefore modest. Left to himself he might have been content to triumph in the reflection that he had failed to say a number of foolish things, but the welfare of his wife and children bound him, tiresomely enough for a dreamer, tightly to the practical. It was clear that if he did not forthwith produce signs of his efficiency as a promoter of the peace that welfare would be imperilled. Yet he did not condemn the

chance that had made him a policeman or
even the mischance that brought no guilty
persons to his hands.   Rather he looked with
a gentle curiosity into the faces of the people
who passed him, and wondered why he could
not detect traces of the generally assumed
wickedness of the neighbourhood.   These
unkempt men and women were thieves and
even murderers, it appeared ; but to him they
shone as happy youths and maidens, joyous
victims of love's tyranny.

As he drew near the street in which he
lived this sense of universal love quickened
in his blood and stirred him strangely.   It
did not escape his eyes that to the general
his uniform was an unfriendly thing.   Men
and women paused in their animated chatter-
ing till he had passed, and even the children
faltered in their games to watch him with
doubtful eyes.   And yet his heart was warm
for them ; he knew that he wished them
well.

Nevertheless, when he saw his house shining
in a row of similar houses, he realised that
their attitude was wiser than his.   If he
was to be a success as a breadwinner he must

wage a sterner war against these happy, lovable people. It was easy, he had been long enough in the force to know how easy, to get cases. An intolerant manner, a little provocative harshness, and the thing was done. Yet with all his heart he admired the poor for their resentful independence of spirit. To him this had always been the supreme quality of the English character; how could he make use of it to fill English gaols?

He opened the door of his house, with a sigh on his lips. There came forth the merry shouting of his children.

II

Above the telephone wires the stars dipped at anchor in the cloudless sky. Down below, in one of the dark, empty streets, Police-constable Bennett turned the handles of doors and tested the fastenings of windows, with a complete scepticism as to the value of his labours. Gradually, he was coming to see that he was not one of the few who are born to rule—to control—their simple neighbours, ambitious only for breath. Where, if he had possessed this mission, he would have been eager to punish, he now felt no more than a sympathy that charged him with some responsibility for the sins of others. He shared the uneasy conviction of the multitude that human justice, as interpreted by the inspired minority, is more than a little unjust. The very unpopularity with which his uniform endowed him seemed to him to express a severe criticism of the system of which he was an unwilling supporter. He wished these people to regard him as a kind of official friend, to advise and settle differences; yet, shrewder than he, they considered him as an enemy, who lived on their mistakes and the collapse of their social relationships.

There remained his duty to his wife and children, and this rendered the problem infinitely perplexing.

Why should he punish others because of his love for his children; or, again, why should his children suffer for his scruples? Yet it was clear that, unless fortune permitted

him to accomplish some notable yet honourable arrest, he would either have to cheat
and tyrannise with his colleagues or leave
the force. And what employment is avail-
able for a discharged policeman?

As he went systematically from house
to house the consideration of these things
marred the normal progress of his dreams.
Conscious as he was of the stars and the
great widths of heaven that made the world
so small, he nevertheless felt that his love
for his family and the wider love that determined his honour were somehow intimately
connected with this greatness of the universe
rather than with the world of little streets
and little motives, and so were not lightly
to be put aside. Yet, how can one measure
one love against another when all are true?

When the door of Gurneys', the money-
lenders, opened to his touch, and drew him
abruptly from his speculations, his first
emotion was a quick irritation that chance
should interfere with his thoughts. But
when his lantern showed him that the lock
had been tampered with, his annoyance
changed to a thrill of hopeful excitement.

What if this were the way out ? What if fate had granted him compromise, the opportunity of pitting his official virtue against official crime, those shadowy forces in the existence of which he did not believe, but which lay on his life like clouds ?

He was not a physical coward, and it seemed quite simple to him to creep quietly through the open door into the silent office without waiting for possible reinforcements. He knew that the safe, which would be the natural goal of the presumed burglars, was in Mr. Gurney's private office beyond, and while he stood listening intently he seemed to hear dim sounds coming from the direction of that room. For a moment he paused, frowning slightly as a man does when he is trying to catalogue an impression. When he achieved perception, it came oddly mingled with recollections of the little tragedies of his children at home. For some one was crying like a child in the little room where Mr. Gurney brow - beat recalcitrant borrowers. Dangerous burglars do not weep, and Bennett hesitated no longer, but stepped past the open

flaps of the counter, and threw open the door
of the inner office.

The electric light had been switched on,
and at the table there sat a slight young man
with his face buried in his hands, crying
bitterly. Behind him the safe stood open and
empty, and the grate was filled with smoulder-
ing embers of burnt paper. Bennett went
up to the young man and placed his hand
on his shoulder. But the young man wept
on and did not move.

Try as he might Bennett could not help
relaxing the grip of outraged law, and patting
the young man's shoulder soothingly as it rose
and fell. He had no fit weapons of rough-
ness and oppression with which to oppose
this child-like grief; he could only fight tears
with tears.

"Come," he said gently, "you must pull
yourself together."

At the sound of his voice the young man
gave a great sob and then was silent, shivering
a little.

"That's better," said Bennett encourag-
ingly, "much better."

"I have burnt everything," the young man

said suddenly, "and now the place is empty. I was nearly sick just now."

Bennett looked at him sympathetically, as one dreamer may look at another, who is sad with action dreamed too often for scatheless accomplishment. "I'm afraid you'll get into serious trouble," he said.

"I know," replied the young man, "but that blackguard Gurney——" His voice rose to a shrill scream and choked him for a moment. Then he went on quietly, "But it's all over now. Finished! Done with!"

"I suppose you owed him money?"

The young man nodded. "He lives on fools like me. But he threatened to tell my father, and now I've just about ruined him. Pah! Swine!"

"This won't be much better for your father," said Bennett gravely.

"No, it's worse; but perhaps it will help some of the others. He kept on threatening and I couldn't wait any longer. Can't you see?"

Over the young man's shoulder the stars becked and nodded to Bennett through the blindless window.

" I see," he said ; " I see."

" So now you can take me."

Bennett looked doubtfully at the out-
stretched wrists. " You are only a fool," he
said, " a dreaming fool like me, and they will
give you years for this. I don't see why they
should give a man years for being a fool."

The young man looked up, taken with a
sudden hope. " You will let me go ? " he
said, in astonishment. " I know I was an ass
just now. I suppose I was a bit shaken. But
you will let me go ? "

" I wish to God I had never seen you ! "
said Bennett simply. " You have your father,
and I have a wife and three little children.
Who shall judge between us ? "

" My father is an old man."

" And my children are little. You had
better go before I make up my mind."

Without another word the young man crept
out of the room, and Bennett followed him
slowly into the street. This gallant criminal,
whose capture would have been honourable,
had dwindled to a hysterical foolish boy ; and
aided by his own strange impulse this boy
had ruined him. The burglary had taken

place on his beat; there would be an inquiry; it did not need that to secure his expulsion from the force.   Once in the street he looked up hopefully to the heavens; but now the stars seemed unspeakably remote, though as he passed along his beat his wife and his three little children were walking by his side.

III

Bennett had developed mentally without realising the logical result of his development until it smote him with calamity.   Of his betrayal of trust as a guardian of property he thought nothing; of the possibility of poverty for his family he thought a great deal—all the more that his dreamer's mind was little accustomed to gripping the practical.   It was strange, he thought, that his final declaration of war against his position should have been a little lacking in dignity. He had not taken the decisive step through any deep compassion of utter poverty bravely borne.   His had been no more than trivial pity of a young man's folly; and this was a frail thing on which to make so great a sacrifice. Yet he regretted nothing. His task of moral guardian of men and women had become impossible to him, and sooner or later he must have given it up. And there was also his family. " I must come to some decision," he said to himself firmly.

And then the great scream fell upon his ears and echoed through his brain for ever and ever. It came from the house before which he was standing, and he expected the whole street to wake aghast with the horror of it. But there followed a silence that seemed to emphasise the ugliness of the sound. Far away an engine screamed as if in mocking imitation ; and that was all. Bennett had counted up to a hundred and seventy before the door of the house opened, and a man came out on to the steps.

" Oh, constable," he said coolly, " come inside, will you ? I have something to show you."

Bennett mounted the steps doubtfully. " There was a scream," he said.

The man looked at him quickly. " So you heard it," he said. " It was not pretty."

" No, it was not," replied Bennett.

The man led him down the dim passage into the back sitting-room. The body of a man lay on the sofa ; it was curled like a dry leaf.

" That is my brother," said the man, with a little emphatic nod ; " I have killed him. He was my enemy."

Bennett stared dully at the body, without believing it to be really there.

" Dead ! " he said mechanically.

" And anything I say will be used against me in evidence ! As if you could compress my hatred into one little lying notebook."

" I don't care a damn about your hatred," said Bennett, with heat. " An hour ago, perhaps, I might have arrested you ; now I only find you uninteresting."

The man gave a long, low whistle of surprise.

" A philosopher in uniform," he said, " God ! sir, you have my sympathy."

" And you have my pity. You have stolen your ideas from cheap melodrama, and you make tragedy ridiculous. Were I a police-man, I would lock you up with pleasure.

Were I a man, I should thrash you joyfully. As it is I can only share your infamy. I too, I suppose, am a murderer."

" You are in a low, nervous state," said the man; "and you are doing me some injustice. It is true that I am a poor murderer; but it appears to me that you are a worse policeman."

" I shall wear the uniform no more from to-night."

" I think you are wise, and I shall mar my philosophy with no more murders. If, indeed, I have killed him; for I assure you that beyond administering the poison to his wretched body I have done nothing. Perhaps he is not dead. Can you hear his heart beating ? "

" I can hear the spoons of my children beating on their empty platters ! "

" Is it like that with you ? Poor devil ! Oh, poor, poor devil ! Philosophers should have no wives, no children, no homes, and no hearts."

Bennett turned from the man with unspeakable loathing.

" I hate you and such as you ! " he cried

weakly. "You justify the existence of the
police. You make me despise myself because
I realise that your crimes are no less mine
than yours. I do not ask you to defend the
deadness of that thing lying there. I shall
stir no finger to have you hanged, for the
thought of suicide repels me, and I cannot
separate your blood and mine. We are
common children of a noble mother, and for
our mother's sake I say farewell."

And without waiting for the man's answer
he passed from the house to the street.

IV

Haggard and with rebellious limbs, Police-
constable Bennett staggered into the superintendent's office in the early morning.

"I have paid careful attention to your
advice," he said to the superintendent, "and
I have passed across the city in search of
crime. In its place I have found but folly—
such folly as you have, such folly as I have
myself—the common heritage of our blood.
It seems that in some way I have bound

myself to bring criminals to justice. I have passed across the city, and I have found no man worse than myself. Do what you will with me."

The superintendent cleared his throat.

" There have been too many complaints concerning the conduct of the police," he said ; " it is time that an example was made. You will be charged with being drunk and disorderly while on duty."

" I have a wife and three little children," said Bennett softly—" and three pretty little children." And he covered his tired face with his hands.

THE CONJURER

CERTAINLY the audience was restive. In the first place it felt that it had been defrauded, seeing that Cissie Bradford, whose smiling face adorned the bills outside, had failed to appear, and secondly, it considered that the deputy for that famous lady was more than inadequate. To the little man who sweated in the glare of the limelight and juggled desperately with glass balls in a vain effort to steady his nerve it was apparent that his turn was a failure. And as he worked he could have cried with disappointment, for his was a trial performance, and a year's engagement in the Hennings' group of music-halls would have rewarded success. Yet his tricks, things that he had done with the utmost ease a thousand times, had been a succession of blunders, rather mirth-provoking than mysti-fying to the audience. Presently one of the glass balls fell crashing on the stage, and amidst the jeers of the gallery he turned to his wife, who served as his assistant.

"I've lost my chance," he said, with a sob; "I can't do it!"

"Never mind, dear," she whispered. "There's a nice steak and onions at home for supper."

"It's no use," he said despairingly. "I'll try the disappearing trick and then get off. I'm done here." He turned back to the audience.

"Ladies and gentlemen," he said to the mockers in a wavering voice, "I will now present to you the concluding item of my entertainment. I will cause this lady to disappear under your very eyes, without the aid of any mechanical contrivance or artificial device." This was the merest showman's patter, for, as a matter of fact, it was not a very wonderful illusion. But as he led his wife forward to present her to the audience the conjurer was wondering whether the mishaps that had ruined his chance would meet him even here. If something should go wrong—he felt his wife's hand tremble in his, and he pressed it

tightly to reassure her. He must make an
effort, an effort of will, and then no mistakes
would happen. For a second the lights danced
before his eyes, then he pulled himself together. If an earthquake should disturb the
curtains and show Molly creeping ignomini-
ously away behind he would still meet his fate
like a man. He turned round to conduct his
wife to the little alcove from which she should
vanish. She was not on the stage!

For a minute he did not guess the greatness
of the disaster. Then he realised that the
theatre was intensely quiet, and that he would
have to explain that the last item of his pro-
gramme was even more of a fiasco than the
rest. Owing to a sudden indisposition—
his skin tingled at the thought of the
hooting. His tongue rasped upon cracking
lips as he braced himself and bowed to the
audience.

Then came the applause. Again and again
it broke out from all over the house, while the
curtain rose and fell, and the conjurer stood
on the stage, mute, uncomprehending. What
had happened ? At first he had thought they
were mocking him, but it was impossible to

misjudge the nature of the applause. Besides, the stage-manager was allowing him call after call, as if he were a star. When at length the curtain remained down, and the orchestra struck up the opening bars of the next song, he staggered off into the wings as if he were drunk. There he met Mr. James Hennings himself.

"You'll do," said the great man; "that last trick was neat. You ought to polish up the others though. I suppose you don't want to tell me how you did it? Well, well, come in the morning and we'll fix up a contract." And so, without having said a word, the conjurer found himself hustled off by the Vaudeville Napoleon. Mr. Hennings had something more to say to his manager.

"Bit rum," he said. "Did you see it?"

"Queerest thing we've struck."

"How was it done do you think?"

"Can't imagine. There one minute on his arm, gone the next, no trap, or curtain, or anything."

"Money in it, eh?"

"Biggest hit of the century, I should think."

" I'll go and fix up a contract and get him to sign it to-night. Get on with it." And Mr. James Hennings fled to his office.

Meanwhile the conjurer was wandering in the wings with the drooping heart of a lost child. What had happened ? Why was he a success, and why did people stare so oddly, and what had become of his wife ? When he asked them the stage hands laughed, and said they had not seen her. Why should they laugh ? He wanted her to explain things, and hear their good luck. But she was not in her dressing-room, she was not anywhere. For a moment he felt like crying.

Then, for the second time that night, he pulled himself together. After all, there was no reason to be upset. He ought to feel very pleased about the contract, however it had happened. It seemed that his wife had left the stage in some queer way without being seen. Probably to increase the mystery she had gone straight home in her stage dress, and had succeeded in dodging the stage-door keeper. It was all very strange ; but, of course, there must be some simple explanation like that. He would take a cab home and

find her there already.   There was a steak
and onions for supper.

As he drove along in the cab he became
convinced that this theory was right.   Molly
had always been clever, and this time she had
certainly succeeded in surprising everybody.
At the door of his house he gave the cabman
a shilling for himself with a light heart.   He
could afford it now.   He ran up the steps
cheerfully and opened the door.   The passage
was quite dark, and he wondered why his wife
hadn't lit the gas.

" Molly ! " he cried, " Molly ! "

The small, weary-eyed servant came out of
the kitchen on a savoury wind of onions.

" Hasn't missus come home with you, sir ? "
she said.

The conjurer thrust his hand against the
wall to steady himself, and the pattern of the
wall-paper seemed to burn his finger-tips.

" Not here ! " he gasped at the frightened
girl.   " Then where is she ?   Where is she ? "

" I don't know, sir," she began stuttering ;
but the conjurer turned quickly and ran out
of the house.   Of course, his wife must be at
the theatre.   It was absurd ever to have

supposed that she could leave the theatre in her stage dress unnoticed; and now she was probably worrying because he had not waited for her. How foolish he had been.

It was a quarter of an hour before he found a cab, and the theatre was dark and empty when he got back to it. He knocked at the stage door, and the night watchman opened it.

" My wife ? " he cried.

" There's no one here now, sir," the man answered respectfully, for he knew that a new star had risen that night.

The conjurer leant against the doorpost faintly.

" Take me up to the dressing-rooms," he said. " I want to see whether she has been there while I was away."

The watchman led the way along the dark passages. " I shouldn't worry if I were you, sir," he said. " She can't have gone far." He did not know anything about it, but he wanted to be sympathetic.

" God knows," the conjurer muttered, " I can't understand this at all."

In the dressing-room Molly's clothes still

lay neatly folded as she had left them when they went on the stage that night, and when he saw them his last hope left the conjurer, and a strange thought came into his mind.

"I should like to go down on the stage," he said, "and see if there is anything to tell me of her."

The night watchman looked at the conjurer as if he thought he was mad, but he followed him down to the stage in silence. When he was there the conjurer leaned forward suddenly, and his face was filled with a wistful eagerness.

"Molly!" he called, "Molly!'

But the empty theatre gave him nothing but echoes in reply.

THE POET'S ALLEGORY

I

THE boy came into the town at six o'clock in the morning, but the baker at the corner of the first street was up, as is the way of bakers, and when he saw the boy passing, he hailed him with a jolly shout.

"Hullo, boy! What are you after?"

"I'm going about my business," the boy said pertly.

"And what might that be, young fellow?"

"I might be a good tinker, and worship god Pan, or I might grind scissors as sharp as the noses of bakers. But, as a matter of fact, I'm a piper, not a rat-catcher, you understand, but just a simple singer of sad songs, and a mad singer of merry ones."

"Oh," said the baker dully, for he had hoped the boy was in search of work. "Then I suppose you have a message."

"I sing songs," the boy said emphatically. "I don't run errands for any one save it be for the fairies."

"Well, then, you have come to tell us that we are bad, that our lives are corrupt and our homes sordid. Nowadays there's money in that if you can do it well."

"Your wit gets up too early in the morning for me, baker," said the boy. "I tell you I sing songs."

"Aye, I know, but there's something in them, I hope. Perhaps you bring news. They're not so popular as the other sort, but still, as long as it's bad news——"

"Is it the flour that has changed his brains to dough, or the heat of the oven that has made them like dead grass?"

"But you must have some news——?"

"News! It's a fine morning of summer, and I saw a kingfisher across the water-meadows coming along. Oh, and there's a cuckoo back in the fir plantation, singing with a May voice. It must have been asleep all these months."

"But, my dear boy, these things happen every day. Are there no battles or earthquakes or famines in the world ? Has no man murdered his wife or robbed his neighbour ? Is no one oppressed by tyrants or lied to by their officers."

The boy shrugged his shoulders.

" I hope not," he said. " But if it were so, and I knew, I should not tell you. I don't want to make you unhappy."

" But of what use are you then, if it be not to rouse in us the discontent that is alone divine ? Would you have me go fat and happy, listening to your babble of kingfishers and cuckoos, while my brothers and sisters in the world are starving ? "

The boy was silent for a moment.

" I give my songs to the poor for nothing," he said slowly. " Certainly they are not much use to empty bellies, but they are all I have to give. And I take it, since you speak so feelingly, that you, too, do your best. And these others, these people who must be reminded hourly to throw their crusts out of window for the poor—would you have me sing to them ? They must be told that life is evil, and I find it good ; that men and women are wretched, and I find them happy ; that food and cleanliness, order and knowledge are the essence of content while I only ask for love.   Would you have me lie to cheat mean folk out of their scraps ? "

The baker scratched his head in astonishment.

" Certainly you are very mad," he said. " But you won't get much money in this town with that sort of talk.   You had better come in and have breakfast with me."

" But why do you ask me ? " said the boy, in surprise.

" Well, you have a decent, honest sort of face, although your tongue is disordered."

" I had rather it had been because you liked my songs," said the boy, and he went in to breakfast with the baker.

II

Over his breakfast the boy talked wisely on art, as is the wont of young singers, and afterwards he went on his way down the street.

" It's a great pity," said the baker; " he seems a decent young chap."

" He has nice eyes," said the baker's wife.

As the boy passed down the street he frowned a little.

" What is the matter with them ? " he wondered. " They're pleasant people enough, and yet they did not want to hear my songs."

Presently he came to the tailor's shop, and as the tailor had sharper eyes than the baker, he saw the pipe in the boy's pocket.

" Hullo, piper ! " he called. " My legs are stiff. Come and sing us a song ! "

The boy looked up and saw the tailor sitting cross-legged in the open window of his shop.

" What sort of song would you like ? " he asked.

" Oh ! the latest," replied the tailor. " We don't want any old songs here." So the boy sung his new song of the kingfisher in the water-meadow and the cuckoo who had over-slept itself.

" And what do you call that ? " asked the tailor angrily, when the boy had finished.

" It's my new song, but I don't think it's one of my best." But in his heart the boy believed it was, because he had only just made it.

"I should hope it's your worst," the tailor said rudely. "What sort of stuff is that to make a man happy?"

"To make a man happy?" echoed the boy, his heart sinking within him.

"If you have no news to give me, why should I pay for your songs? I want to hear about my neighbours, about their lives, and their wives and their sins. There's the fat baker up the street—they say he cheats the poor with light bread. Make me a song of that, and I'll give you some breakfast. Or there's the magistrate at the top of the hill who made the girl drown herself last week. That's a poetic subject."

"What's all this?" said the boy disdainfully. "Can't you make dirt enough for yourself?"

"You with your stuff about birds," shouted the tailor; "you're a rank impostor! That's what you are!"

"They say that you are the ninth part of a man, but I find that they have grossly exaggerated," cried the boy, in retort; but he had a heavy heart as he made off along the street.

By noon he had interviewed the butcher, the cobbler, the milkman, and the maker of candlesticks, but they treated him no better than the tailor had done, and as he was feeling tired he went and sat down under a tree.

" I begin to think that the baker is the best of the lot of them," he said to himself ruefully, as he rolled his empty wallet between his fingers.

Then, as the folly of singers provides them in some measure with a philosophy, he fell asleep.

III

When he woke it was late in the afternoon, and the children, fresh from school, had come out to play in the dusk. Far and near, across the town-square, the boy could hear their merry voices, but he felt sad, for his stomach had forgotten the baker's breakfast, and he did not see where he was likely to get any supper. So he pulled out his pipe, and made a mournful song to himself of the dancing gnats and the bitter odour of the bonfires in the townsfolk's gardens. And the children drew near to hear him sing, for they thought his song was pretty, until their fathers drove them home, saying, " That stuff has no educational value."

" Why haven't you a message ?" they asked the boy.

" I come to tell you that the grass is green beneath your feet and that the sky is blue over your heads."

" Oh ! but we know all that," they answered.

" Do you ! Do you ! " screamed the boy. " Do you think you could stop over your absurd labours if you knew how blue the sky is ? You would be out singing on the hills with me ! "

" Then who would do our work ? " they said, mocking him.

" Then who would want it done ? " he retorted ; but it's ill arguing on an empty stomach.

But when they had tired of telling him what a fool he was, and gone away, the tailor's little daughter crept out of the shadows and patted him on the shoulder.

"I say, boy!" she whispered. "I've brought you some supper. Father doesn't know." The boy blessed her and ate his supper while she watched him like his mother and when he had done she kissed him on the lips.

"There, boy!" she said.

"You have nice golden hair," the boy said. "See! it shines in the dusk. It strikes me it's the only gold I shall get in this town."

"Still it's nice, don't you think?" the girl whispered in his ear. She had her arms round his neck.

"I love it," the boy said joyfully; "and you like my songs, don't you?"

"Oh, yes, I like them very much, but I like you better."

The boy put her off roughly.

"You're as bad as the rest of them," he said indignantly. "I tell you my songs are everything, I am nothing."

"But it was you who ate my supper, boy," said the girl.

The boy kissed her remorsefully. "But I wish you had liked me for my songs," he sighed.

"You are better than any silly old songs!"

"As bad as the rest of them," the boy said lazily, "but somehow pleasant."

The shadows flocked to their evening meeting in the square, and overhead the stars shone out in a sky that was certainly exceedingly blue.

IV

Next morning they arrested the boy as a rogue and a vagabond, and in the afternoon they brought him before the magistrate.

"And what have you to say for yourself?" said the magistrate to the boy, after the second policeman, like a faithful echo, had finished reading his notes.

"Well," said the boy, "I may be a rogue and a vagabond. Indeed, I think that I probably am; but I would claim the license that has always been allowed to singers."

"Oh!" said the magistrate. "So you are one of those, are you? And what is your message?"

"I think if I could sing you a song or two I could explain myself better," said the boy.

" Well," replied the magistrate doubtfully, "you can try if you like, but I warn you that I wrote songs myself when I was a boy, so that I know something about it."

" Oh, I'm glad of that," said the boy, and he sang his famous song of the grass that is so green, and when he had finished the magistrate frowned.

" I knew that before," he said.

So then the boy sang his wonderful song of the sky that is so blue. And when he had finished the magistrate scowled. " And what are we to learn from that ? " he said.

So then the boy lost his temper and sang some naughty doggerel he had made up in his cell that morning. He abused the town and townsmen, but especially the townsmen. He damned their morals, their customs, and their institutions. He said that they had ugly faces, raucous voices, and that their bodies were unclean. He said they were thieves and liars and murderers, that they had no ear for music and no sense of humour. Oh, he was bitter !

" Good God ! " said the magistrate, " that's what I call real improving poetry. Why didn't you sing that first? There might have been a miscarriage of justice."

Then the baker, the tailor, the butcher, the cobbler, the milkman, and the maker of candlesticks rose in court and said—

" Ah, but we all knew there was something in him."

So the magistrate gave the boy a certificate that showed that he was a real singer, and the tradesmen gave him a purse of gold, but the tailor's little daughter gave him one of her golden ringlets. " You won't forget, boy, will you ? " she said.

" Oh, no," said the boy; "but I wish you had liked my songs."

Presently, when he had come a little way out of the town, he put his hand in his wallet and drew out the magistrate's certificate and tore it in two; and then he took out the gold pieces and threw them into the ditch, and they were not half as bright as the buttercups. But when he came to the ringlet he smiled at it and put it back.

" Yet she was as bad as the rest of them," he thought with a sigh.

And he went across the world with his songs.

AND WHO SHALL SAY——?

IT was a dull November day, and the windows
were heavily curtained, so that the room was
very dark. In front of the fire was a large
arm-chair, which shut whatever light there
might be from the two children, a boy of
eleven and a girl about two years younger,
who sat on the floor at the back of the room.

The boy was the better looking, but the
girl had the better face. They were both
gazing at the arm-chair with the utmost
excitement.

" It's all right. He's asleep," said the boy.

" Oh, do be careful ! you'll wake him," whispered the girl.

" Are you afraid ? "

" No, why should I be afraid of my father,
stupid ? "

" I tell you he's not father any more. He's
a murderer," the boy said hotly. " He told

me, I tell you. He said, ' I have killed your mother, Ray,' and I went and looked, and mother was all red. I simply shouted, and she wouldn't answer. That means she's dead. His hand was all red, too."

" Was it paint ? "

" No, of course it wasn't paint. It was blood. And then he came down here and went to sleep."

" Poor father, so tired."

" He's not poor father, he's not father at all; he's a murderer, and it is very wicked of you to call him father," said the boy.

" Father," muttered the girl rebelliously.

" You know the sixth commandment says ' Thou shalt do no murder,' and he has done murder ; so he'll go to hell. And you'll go to hell too if you call him father. It's all in the Bible."

The boy ended vaguely, but the little girl was quite overcome by the thought of her badness.

" Oh, I am wicked !" she cried. " And I do so want to go to heaven."

She had a stout and materialistic belief in it as a place of sheeted angels and harps, where it was easy to be good.

" You must do as I tell you, then," he said.
" Because I know.   I've learnt all about it at
school."

"And you never told me," said she reproach-
fully.

" Ah, there's lots of things I know," he
replied, nodding his head.

" What must we do ? " said the girl meekly.
" Shall I go and ask mother ? "

The boy was sick at her obstinacy.

" Mother's dead, I tell you ; that means she
can't hear anything.   It's no use talking to
her; but I know.   You must stop here, and if
father wakes you run out of the house and
call ' Police!' and I will go now and tell a
policeman I know."

" And what happens then ? " she asked,
with round eyes at her brother's wisdom.

" Oh, they come and take him away to
prison.   And then they put a rope round his
neck and hang him like Haman, and he goes
to hell."

" Wha-at !   Do they kill him ? "

"Because he's a murderer.   They always do."

" Oh, don't let's tell them !   Don't let's tell
them ! " she screamed.

"Shut up!" said the boy, "or he'll wake up. We must tell them, or we go to hell— both of us."

But his sister did not collapse at this awful threat, as he expected, though the tears were rolling down her face. "Don't let's tell them," she sobbed.

"You're a horrid girl, and you'll go to hell," said the boy, in disgust. But the silence was only broken by her sobbing. "I tell you he killed mother dead. You didn't cry a bit for mother; I did."

"Oh, let's ask mother! Let's ask mother! I know she won't want father to go to hell. Let's ask mother!"

"Mother's dead, and can't hear, you stupid," said the boy. "I keep on telling you. Come up and look."

They were both a little awed in mother's room. It was so quiet, and mother looked so funny. And first the girl shouted, and then the boy, and then they shouted both together, but nothing happened. The echoes made them frightened.

"Perhaps she's asleep," the girl said; so her brother pinched one of mother's hands—the white one, not the red one—but nothing happened, so mother was dead.

"Has she gone to hell?" whispered the girl.

"No! she's gone to heaven, because she's good. Only wicked people go to hell. And now I must go and tell the policeman. Don't you tell father where I've gone if he wakes up, or he'll run away before the policeman comes."

"Why?"

"So as not to go to hell," said the boy, with certainty; and they went downstairs together, the little mind of the girl being much perturbed because she was so wicked. What would mother say to-morrow if she had done wrong?

The boy put on his sailor hat in the hall. "You must go in there and watch," he said, nodding in the direction of the sitting-room. "I shall run all the way."

The door banged, and she heard his steps down the path, and then everything was quiet.

She tiptoed into the room, and sat down on the floor, and looked at the back of the chair in utter distress. She could see her father's elbow projecting on one side, but nothing more. For an instant she hoped that he wasn't there—hoped that he had gone—but then, terrified, she knew that this was a piece of extreme wickedness.

So she lay on the rough carpet, sobbing hopelessly, and seeing real and vicious devils of her brother's imagining in all the corners of the room.

Presently, in her misery, she remembered a packet of acid-drops that lay in her pocket, and drew them forth in a sticky mass, which parted from its paper with regret. So she choked and sucked her sweets at the same time, and found them salt and tasteless.

Ray was gone a long time, and she was a wicked girl who would go to hell if she didn't do what he told her. Those were her prevailing ideas.

And presently there came a third. Ray had said that if her father woke up he would run away, and not go to hell at all. Now if she woke him up——.

She knew this was dreadfully naughty ; but her mind clung to the idea obstinately. You see, father had always been so fond of mother, and he would not like to be in a different

place. Mother wouldn't like it either. She
was always so sorry when father did not come
home or anything. And hell is a dreadful
place, full of things. She half convinced herself, and started up, but then there came an
awful thought.

If she did this she would go to hell for ever
and ever, and all the others would be in
heaven.

She hung there in suspense, sucking her
sweet and puzzling it over with knit brows.

How can one be good?

She swung round and looked in the dark
corner by the piano; but the Devil was not
there.

And then she ran across the room to her
father, and shaking his arm, shouted, tremu-
lously—

"Wake up, father! Wake up! The police
are coming!"

And when the police came ten minutes
later, accompanied by a very proud and
virtuous little boy, they heard a small shrill
voice crying, despairingly—

"The police, father! The police!"

But father would not wake.

THE BIOGRAPHY OF A SUPER-MAN

"O limèd soul that struggling to be free
Art more engaged!"

CHARLES STEPHEN DALE, the subject of my
study, was a dramatist and, indeed, something of a celebrity in the early years of
the twentieth century. That he should be
already completely forgotten is by no means
astonishing in an age that elects its great men
with a charming indecision of touch. The
general prejudice against the granting of free-
holds has spread to the desired lands of fame ;
and where our profligate ancestors were willing
to call a man great in perpetuity, we, with
more shrewdness, prefer to name him a genius
for seven years. We know that before that
period may have expired fate will have granted
us a sea-serpent with yet more coils, with a

yet more bewildering arrangement of marine and sunset tints, and the conclusion of previous leases will enable us to grant him undisputed possession of Parnassus. If our ancestors were more generous they were certainly less discriminate ; and it cannot be doubted that many of them went to their graves under the impression that it is possible for there to be more than one great man at a time ! We have altered all that.

For two years Dale was a great man, or rather the great man, and it is probable that if he had not died he would have held his position for a longer period. When his death was announced, although the notices of his life and work were of a flattering length, the leader-writers were not unnaturally aggrieved that he should have resigned his post before the popular interest in his personality was exhausted. The Censor might do his best by prohibiting the performance of all the plays that the dead man had left behind him ; but, as the author neglected to express his views in their columns, and the common sense of their readers forbade the publication of interviews with him, the journals could draw but a poor satisfaction from condemning or upholding the official action. Dale's regrettable absence reduced what might have been an agreeable clash of personalities to an arid discussion on art. The consequence was obvious. The end of the week saw the elevation of James Macintosh, the great Scotch comedian, to the vacant post, and Dale was completely forgotten. That this oblivion is merited in terms of his work I am not prepared to admit ; that it is merited in terms of his personality I indignantly wish to deny. Whatever Dale may have been as an artist, he was, perhaps in spite of himself, a man, and a man moreover, possessed of many striking and unusual traits of character. It is to the man Dale that I offer this tribute.

Sprung from an old Yorkshire family, Charles Stephen Dale was yet sufficient of a Cockney to justify both his friends and his enemies in crediting him with the Celtic temperament. Nevertheless, he was essentially a modern, insomuch that his contempt for the writings of dead men surpassed his dislike of living authors. To these two central influences we may trace most of the peculiarities that rendered him notorious and ultimately great. Thus, while his Celtic æstheticism permitted him to eat nothing but raw meat, because he mistrusted alike " the reeking products of the manure-heap and the barbaric fingers of cooks," it was surely his modernity that made him an agnostic, because bishops sat in the House of Lords. Smaller men might dislike vegetables and bishops without allowing it to affect their conduct; but Dale was careful to observe that every slightest conviction should have its place in the formation of his character. Conversely, he was nothing without a reason.

These may seem small things to which to trace the motive forces of a man's life; but if we add to them a third, found where the truth about a man not infrequently lies, in the rag-bag of his enemies, our materials will be nearly complete. "Dale hates his fellow-human-beings," wrote some anonymous scribbler, and, even expressed thus baldly, the statement is not wholly false. But he hated them because of their imperfections, and it would be truer to say that his love of humanity amounted to a positive hatred of

individuals, and, *pace* the critics, the love was
no less sincere than the hatred. He had
drawn from the mental confusion of the
darker German philosophers an image of the
perfect man—an image differing only in in-
essentials from the idol worshipped by the
Imperialists as " efficiency." He did not
find—it was hardly likely that he would
find—that his contemporaries fulfilled this
perfect conception, and he therefore felt it
necessary to condemn them for the possession of those weaknesses, or as some would
prefer to say qualities, of which the sum is
human nature.

I now approach a quality, or rather the
lack of a quality, that is in itself of so
debatable a character, that were it not of the
utmost importance in considering the life of
Charles Stephen Dale I should prefer not to
mention it. I refer to his complete lack of a
sense of humour, the consciousness of which
deficiency went so far to detract from his
importance as an artist and a man. The
difficulty which I mentioned above lies in the
fact that, while every one has a clear conception of what they mean by the phrase, no one

has yet succeeded in defining it satisfactorily. Here I would venture to suggest that it is a kind of magnificent sense of proportion, a sense that relates the infinite greatness of the universe to the finite smallness of man, and draws the inevitable conclusion as to the importance of our joys and sorrows and labours. I am aware that this definition errs on the side of vagueness; but possibly it may be found to include the truth. Obviously, the natures of those who possess this sense will tend to be static rather than dynamic, and it is therefore against the limits imposed by this sense that intellectual anarchists, among whom I would number Dale, and poets primarily rebel. But—and it is this rather than his un-doubted intellectual gifts or his dogmatic definitions of good and evil that definitely separated Dale from the normal men—there can be no doubt that he felt his lack of a sense of humour bitterly. In every word he ever said, in every line he ever wrote, I detect a painful striving after this mysterious sense, that enabled his neighbours, fools as he un-doubtedly thought them, to laugh and weep and follow the faith of their hearts without conscious realisation of their own existence and the problems it induced. By dint of study and strenuous observation he achieved, as any man may achieve, a considerable degree of wit, though to the last his ignorance of the audience whom he served and despised, prevented him from judging the effect of his sallies without experiment. But try as he might the finer jewel lay far beyond his reach. Strong men fight themselves when they can find no fitter adversary ; but in all the history of literature there is no stranger spectacle than this lifelong contest between Dale, the intellectual anarch and pioneer of supermen, and Dale, the poor lonely devil who wondered what made people happy.

I have said that the struggle was lifelong, but it must be added that it was always unequal. The knowledge that in his secret heart he desired this quality, the imperfection of imperfections, only served to make Dale's attack on the complacency of his contemporaries more bitter. He ridiculed their achievements, their ambitions, and their love with a fury that awakened in them a mild curiosity, but by no means affected their comfort. Moreover, the very vehemence with which he demanded their contempt deprived him of much of his force as a critic, for they justly wondered why a man should waste his lifetime in attacking them if they were indeed so worthless. Actually, they felt, Dale was a great deal more engaged with his audience than many of the imaginative writers whom he affected to despise for their sycophancy. And, especially towards the end of his life when his powers perhaps were weakening, the devices which he used to arouse the irritation of his contemporaries became more and more childishly artificial, less and less effective. He was like one of those actors who feel that they cannot hold the attention of their audience unless they are always doing something, though nothing is more monotonous than mannered vivacity.

Dale, then, was a man who was very anxious to be modern, but at the same time had not wholly succeeded in conquering his æsthetic sense. He had constituted himself high priest of the most puritanical and remote of all creeds, yet there was that in his blood that rebelled ceaselessly against the intellectual limits he had voluntarily accepted. The result in terms of art was chaos. Possessed of an intellect of great analytic and destructive force, he was almost entirely lacking in imagination, and he was therefore unable to raise his work to a plane in which the mutually combative elements of his nature might have been reconciled. His light moments of envy, anger, and vanity passed into the crucible to come forth unchanged. He lacked the magic wand, and his work never took wings above his conception. It is in vain to seek in any of his plays or novels, tracts or prefaces, for the product of inspiration, the divine gift that enables one man to write with the common pen of humanity. He could only employ his curiously perfect technique in reproducing the wayward flashes of a mind incapable of consecutive thought. He never attempted—and this is a hard saying—to produce any work beautiful in itself; while the confusion of his mind, and the vanity that never allowed him to ignore the effect his work might produce on his audience, prevented him from giving clear expression to his creed. His work will appeal rather to the student of men than to the student of art, and, wantonly incoherent though it often is, must be held to constitute a remarkable human document.

It is strange to reflect that among his contemporary admirers Dale was credited with an intellect of unusual clarity, for the examination of any of his plays impresses one with the number and mutual destructiveness of his motives for artistic expression. A noted debater, he made frequent use of the device of attacking the weakness of the other man's speech, rather than the weakness of the other man's argument. His prose was good, though at its best so impersonal that it recalled the manner of an exceptionally well-written leading article. At its worst it was marred by numerous vulgarities and errors of taste, not always, it is to be feared, intentional. His attitude on this point was typical of his strange blindness to the necessity of a pure artistic ideal. He committed these extravagances, he would say, in order to irritate his audience into a condition of mental alertness. As a matter of fact, he generally made his readers more sorry than angry, and he did not realise that even if he had been successful it was but a poor reward for the wanton spoiling of much good work. He proclaimed himself to be above criticism, but he was only too often beneath it. Revolting against the dignity, not infrequently pompous, of his fellowmen of letters, he played the part of clown with more enthusiasm than skill. It is intellectual arrogance in a clever man to believe that he can play the fool with success merely because he wishes it.

There is no need for me to enter into detail with regard to Dale's personal appearance; the caricaturists did him rather more than justice, the photographers rather less. In his younger days he suggested a gingerbread man that had been left too long in the sun; towards the end he affected a cultured and elaborate ruggedness that made him look like a duke or a market gardener. Like most clever men, he had good eyes.

Nor is it my purpose to add more than a word to the published accounts of his death. There is something strangely pitiful in that last desperate effort to achieve humour. We have all read the account of his own death that he dictated from the sick-bed—cold, epigrammatic, and, alas! characteristically lacking in taste. And once more it was his fate to make us rather sorry than angry.

In the third scene of the second act of " Henry V.," a play written by an author whom Dale pretended to despise, Dame Quickly describes the death of Falstaff in words that are too well known to need quotation. It was thus and no otherwise that Dale died. It is thus that every man dies.

BLUE BLOOD

HE sat in the middle of the great café with his head supported on his hands, miserable even to bitterness. Inwardly he cursed the ancestors who had left him little but a great name and a small and ridiculous body. He thought of his father, whose expensive eccentricities had amused his fellow-countrymen at the cost of his fortune; his mother, for whom death had been a blessing; his grandparents and his uncles, in whom no man had found any good. But most of all he cursed himself, for whose follies even heredity might not wholly account. He recalled the school where he had made no friends, the University where he had taken no degree. Since he had left Oxford, his aimless, hopeless life, profligate, but dishonourable, perhaps, only by accident, had deprived even his title of any social value, and one by one his very acquaintances had left him to the society of broken men and the women who are anything but light. And these, and here perhaps the root of his bitterness lay, even these recognised him only as a victim for their mockery, a thing more poor than themselves, whereon they could satisfy the anger of their tortured souls. And his last misery lay in this : that he himself could find no day in his life to admire, no one past dream to cherish, no inmost corner of his heart to love. The lowest tramp, the least-heeded waif of the night, might have some ultimate pride, but he himself had nothing, nothing whatever. He was a dream-pauper, an emotional bankrupt.

With a choked sob he drained his brandy and told the waiter to bring him another. There had been a period in his life when he had been able to find some measure of sentimental satisfaction in the stupor of drunkenness. In those days, through the veil of illusion which alcohol had flung across his brain, he had been able to regard the contempt of the men as the intimacy of friendship, the scorn of the women as the laughter

of light love. But now drink gave him
nothing but the mordant insight of mor-
bidity, which cut through his rotten soul
like cheese. Yet night after night he came
to this place, to be tortured afresh by the
ridicule of the sordid frequenters, and by
the careless music of the orchestra which
told him of a flowerless spring and of a
morning which held for him no hope. For
his last emotion rested in this self-inflicted
pain; he could only breathe freely under the
lash of his own contempt.

Idly he let his dull eyes stray about the
room, from table to table, from face to face.
Many there he knew by sight, from none
could he hope for sympathy or even com-
panionship. In his bitterness he envied the
courage of the cowards who were brave
enough to seek oblivion or punishment in
death. Dropping his eyes to his soft, unlovely hands, he marvelled that anything
so useless should throb with life, and yet
he realised that he was afraid of physical
pain, terrified at the thought of death.
There were dim ancestors of his whose
valour had thrilled the songs of minstrels

and made his name lovely in the glowing
folly of battles. But now he knew that he
was a coward, and even in the knowledge
he could find no comfort. It is not given
to every man to hate himself gladly.

The music and the laughter beat on his
sullen brain with a mocking insistence, and
he trembled with impotent anger at the apparent happiness of humanity. Why should
these people be merry when he was miserable, what right had the orchestra to play
a chorus of triumph over the stinging em-
blems of his defeat? He drank brandy after
brandy, vainly seeking to dull the nausea of
disgust which had stricken his worn nerves;
but the adulterated spirit merely maddened
his brain with the vision of new depths of
horror, while his body lay below, a mean,
detestable thing. Had he known how to
pray he would have begged that something
might snap. But no man may win to faith
by means of hatred alone, and his heart was
cold as the marble table against which he
leant. There was no more hope in the
world. . . .

When he came out of the café, the air of

the night was so pure and cool on his face,
and the lights of the square were so tender to
his eyes, that for a moment his harsh mood
was softened.   And in that moment he
seemed to see among the crowd that
flocked by a beautiful face, a face touched
with pearls, and the inner leaves of pink
rosebuds. He leant forward eagerly. " Christine ! " he cried, " Christine ! "

Then the illusion passed, and, smitten by the
anger of the pitiless stars, he saw that he was
looking upon a mere woman, a woman of the
earth.   He fled from her smile with a shudder.

As he went it seemed to him that the
swaying houses buffeted him about as a
child might play with a ball. Sometimes they
threw him against men, who cursed him and
bruised his soft body with their fists.   Sometimes they tripped him up and hurled him
upon the stones of the pavement. Still he
held on, till the Embankment broke before
him with the sudden peace of space, and he
leant against the parapet, panting and sick
with pain, but free from the tyranny of the
houses.

Beneath him the river rolled towards the

sea, reticent but more alive, it seemed, than the deeply painful thing which fate had attached to his brain. He pictured himself tangled in the dark perplexity of its waters, he fancied them falling upon his face like a girl's hair, till they darkened his eyes and choked the mouth which, even now, could not breathe fast enough to satisfy him. The thought displeased him, and he turned away from the place that held peace for other men but not for him. From the shadow of one of the seats a woman's voice reached him, begging peevishly for money.

"I have none," he said automatically. Then he remembered and flung coins, all the money he had, into her lap. "I give it to you because I hate you!" he shrieked, and hurried on lest her thanks should spoil his spite.

Then the black houses and the warped streets had him in their grip once more, and sported with him till his consciousness waxed to one white-hot point of pain. Overhead the stars were laughing quietly in the fields of space, and sometimes a policeman or a chance passer-by looked curiously at his lurching figure, but he only knew that life was hurting him beyond endurance, and that he yet endured. Up and down the ice-cold corridors of his brain, thought, formless and timeless, passed like a rodent flame. Now he was the universe, a vast thing loathsome with agony, now he was a speck of dust, an atom whose infinite torment was imperceptible even to God. Always there was something—something conscious of the intolerable evil called life, something that cried bitterly to be uncreated. Always, while his soul beat against the bars, his body staggered along the streets, a thing helpless, unguided.

There is an hour before dawn when tired men and women die, and with the coming of this hour his spirit found a strange release from pain. Once more he realised that he was a man, and, bruised and weary as he was, he tried to collect the lost threads of reason, which the night had torn from him. Facing him he saw a vast building dimly outlined against the darkness, and in some way it served to touch a faint memory in his dying brain. For a while he wandered amongst the shadows, and then he knew that it was the keep of a castle, his castle, and that high up where a window shone upon the night a girl was waiting for him, a girl with a face of pearls and roses. Presently she came to the window and looked out, dressed all in white for her love's sake. He stood up in his armour and flashed his sword towards the envying stars.

"It is I, my love!" he cried. "I am here."

And there, before the dawn had made the shadows of the Law Courts grey, they found him; bruised and muddy and daubed with blood, without the sword and spurs of his honour, lacking the scented token of his love. A thing in no way tragic, for here was no misfortune, but merely the conclusion of Nature's remorseless logic. For century after century those of his name had lived, sheltered by the prowess of their ancestors from the trivial hardships and afflictions that make us men. And now he lay on the pavement, stiff and cold, a babe that had cried itself to sleep because it could not understand, silent until the morning.

FATE AND THE ARTIST

THE workmen's dwellings stood in the north-west of London, in quaint rivalry with the comfortable ugliness of the Maida Vale blocks of flats. They were fairly new and very well built, with wide stone staircases that echoed all day to the impatient footsteps of children, and with a flat roof that served at once as a playground for them and a drying-ground for their mothers' washing. In hot weather it was pleasant enough to play hide-and-seek or follow-my-leader up and down the long alleys of cool white linen, and if a sudden gust of wind or some unexpected turn of the game set the wet sheets flapping in the children's faces, their senses were rather tickled than annoyed.

To George, mooning in a corner of the railings that seemed to keep all London in a cage, these games were hardly more im-

portant than the shoutings and whistlings
that rose from the street below. It seemed to
him that all his life—he had lived eleven years
—he had been standing in a corner watching
other people engaging in meaningless ploys
and antics. The sun was hot, and yet the
children ran about and made themselves hotter,
and he wondered, as when he had been in
bed with one of his frequent illnesses he had
wondered at the grown-up folk who came and
went, moving their arms and legs and speaking
with their mouths, when it was possible to lie
still and quiet and feel the moments ticking
themselves off in one's forehead. As he rested
in his corner, he was conscious of the sharp
edge of the narrow stone ledge on which he
was sitting and the thin iron railings that
pressed into his back; he smelt the evil smell
of hot London, and the soapy odour of the
washing; he saw the glitter of the dust, and
the noises of the place beat harshly upon his
ears, but he could find no meaning in it all.
Life spoke to him with a hundred tongues,
and all the while he was longing for silence.
To the older inhabitants of the tenements he
seemed a morbid little boy, unhappily too

delicate for sense to be safely knocked into him; his fellow-children would have ignored him completely if he had not had strange fancies that made interesting stories and sometimes inspired games. On the whole, George was lonely without knowing what loneliness meant.

All day long the voice of London throbbed up beyond the bars, and George would regard the chimneys and the housetops and the section of lively street that fell within his range with his small, keen eyes, and wonder why the world did not forthwith crumble into silent, peaceful dust, instead of groaning and quivering in continual unrest. But when twilight fell and the children were tired of playing, they would gather round him in his corner by the tank and ask him to tell them stories. This tank was large and open and held rain water for the use of the tenants, and originally it had been cut off from the rest of the roof by some special railings of its own; but two of the railings had been broken, and now the children could creep through and sit round the tank at dusk, like Eastern villagers round the village well.

And George would tell them stories—queer stories with twisted faces and broken backs, that danced and capered merrily enough as a rule, but sometimes stood quite still and made horrible grimaces. The children liked the cheerful moral stories better, such as Arthur's Boots.

"Once upon a time," George would begin, "there was a boy called Arthur, who lived in a house like this, and always tied his bootlaces with knots instead of bows. One night he stood on the roof and wished he had wings like a sparrow, so that he could fly away over the houses. And a great wind began, so that everybody said there was a storm, and suddenly Arthur found he had a little pair of wings, and he flew away with the wind over the houses. And presently he got beyond the storm to a quiet place in the sky, and Arthur looked up and saw all the stars tied to heaven with little bits of string, and all the strings were tied in bows. And this was done so that God could pull the string quite easily when He wanted to, and let the stars fall. On fine nights you can see them dropping. Arthur thought that the angels must have very neat fingers to tie so many bows, but suddenly, while he was looking, his feet began to feel heavy, and he stooped down to take off his boots ; but he could not untie the knots quick enough, and soon he started falling very fast. And while he was falling, he heard the wind in the telegraph wires, and the shouts of the boys who sell papers in the street, and then he fell on the top of a house.   And they took him to the hospital, and cut off his legs, and gave him wooden ones instead.   But he could not fly any more because they were too heavy."

For days afterwards all the children would tie their bootlaces in bows.

Sometimes they would all look into the dark tank, and George would tell them about the splendid fish that lived in its depths.   If the tank was only half full, he would whisper to the fish, and the children would hear its indistinct reply.   But when the tank was full to the brim, he said that the fish was too happy to talk, and he would describe the beauty of its appearance so vividly that all the children would lean over the tank and strain their eyes in a desperate effort to see the wonderful fish.   But no one ever saw it clearly except George, though most of the children thought they had seen its tail disappearing in the shadows at one time or another.

It was doubtful how far the children believed his stories; probably, not having acquired the habit of examining evidence, they were content to accept ideas that threw a pleasant glamour on life.   But the coming of Jimmy Simpson altered this agreeable condition of mind.   Jimmy was one of those masterful stupid boys who excel at games and physical contests, and triumph over intellectual problems by sheer braggart ignorance. From the first he regarded George with contempt, and when he heard him telling his stories he did not conceal his disbelief.

" It's a lie," he said; " there ain't no fish in the tank."

" I have seen it, I tell you," said George.

Jimmy spat on the asphalt rudely.

" I bet no one else has," he said.

George looked round his audience, but their eyes did not meet his.   They felt that they might have been mistaken in believing that

they had seen the tail of the fish. And Jimmy
was a very good man with his fists. "Liar!"
said Jimmy at last triumphantly, and walked
away. Being masterful, he led the others with
him, and George brooded by the tank for the
rest of the evening in solitude.

Next day George went up to Jimmy con-
fidently. "I was right about the fish," he
said. "I dreamed about it last night."

"Rot!" said Jimmy; "dreams are only
made-up things; they don't mean anything."

George crept away sadly. How could he
convince such a man? All day long he
worried over the problem, and he woke up
in the middle of the night with it throbbing
in his brain. And suddenly, as he lay in his
bed, doubt came to him. Supposing he had
been wrong, supposing he had never seen the
fish at all? This was not to be borne. He
crept quietly out of the flat, and tiptoed upstairs to the roof. The stone was very cold to
his feet.

There were so many things in the tank that
at first George could not see the fish, but at
last he saw it gleaming below the moon and
the stars, larger and even more beautiful than

he had said. " I knew I was right," he whispered, as he crept back to bed.   In the
morning he was very ill.

Meanwhile blue day succeeded blue day,
and while the water grew lower in the tank,
the children, with Jimmy for leader, had
almost forgotten the boy who had told them
stories.   Now and again one or other of them
would say that George was very, *very* ill, and
then they would go on with their game.   No
one looked in the tank now that they knew
there was nothing in it, till it occurred one
day to Jimmy that the dry weather should
have brought final confirmation of his scepticism.   Leaving his comrades at the long
jump, he went to George's neglected corner
and peeped into the tank.   Sure enough it
was almost dry, and, he nearly shouted with
surprise, in the shallow pool of sooty water
there lay a large fish, dead, but still gleaming
with rainbow colours.

Jimmy was strong and stupid, but not ill-
natured, and, recalling George's illness, it
occurred to him that it would be a decent
thing to go and tell him he was right.   He
ran downstairs and knocked on the door of

the flat where George lived. George's big
sister opened it, but the boy was too excited
to see that her eyes were wet. " Oh, miss,"
he said breathlessly, "tell George he was
right about the fish. I've seen it myself ! "

" Georgy's dead," said the girl.

THE GREAT MAN

To the people who do not write it must seem
odd that men and women should be willing to
sacrifice their lives in the endeavour to find
new arrangements and combinations of words
with which to express old thoughts and older
emotions, yet that is not an unfair statement
of the task of the literary artist. Words—
symbols that represent the noises that human
beings make with their tongues and lips and
teeth—lie within our grasp like the fragments
of a jig-saw puzzle, and we fit them into faulty
pictures until our hands grow weary and our
eyes can no longer pretend to see the truth.
In order to illustrate an infinitesimal fraction
of our lives by means of this preposterous
game we are willing to sacrifice all the rest.
While ordinary efficient men and women are
enjoying the promise of the morning, the

fulfilment of the afternoon, the tranquillity of
evening, we are still trying to discover a
fitting epithet for the dew of dawn.   For us
Spring paves the woods with beautiful words
rather than flowers, and when we look into
the eyes of our mistress we see nothing but
adjectives.   Love is an occasion for songs;
Death but the overburdened father of all our
saddest phrases.   We are of those who are
born crying into the world because they
cannot speak, and we end, like Stevenson, by
looking forward to our death because we have
written a good epitaph.   Sometimes in the
course of our frequent descents from heaven
to the waste-paper basket we feel that we lose
too much to accomplish so little.   Does a
handful of love-songs really outweigh the
smile of a pretty girl, or a hardly-written
romance compensate the author for months of
lost adventure?   We have only one life to
live, and we spend the greater part of it
writing the history of dead hours.   Our lives
lack balance because we find it hard to discover a mean between the triolet we wrote last
night and the big book we are going to start
to-morrow, and also because living only with

our heads we tend to become top-heavy. We justify our present discomfort with the promise of a bright future of flowers and sunshine and gladdest life, though we know that in the garden of art there are many chrysalides and few butterflies. Few of us are fortunate enough to accomplish anything that was in the least worth doing, so we fall back on the arid philosophy that it is effort alone that counts.

Luckily—or suicide would be the rule rather than the exception for artists—the long process of disillusionment is broken by hours when even the most self-critical feel nobly and indubitably great ; and this is the only reward that most artists ever have for their labours, if we set a higher price on art than money. On the whole, I am inclined to think that the artist is fully rewarded, for the common man can have no conception of the joy that is to be found in belonging, though but momentarily and illusively, to the aristocracy of genius. To find the just word for all our emotions, to realise that our most trivial thought is illimitably creative, to feel that it is our lot to keep life's gladdest promises, to

see the great souls of men and women, stead-
fast in existence as stars in a windless pool—
these, indeed, are no ordinary pleasures.
Moreover, these hours of our illusory greatness endow us in their passing with a melancholy that is not tainted with bitterness. We
have nothing to regret; we are in truth the
richer for our rare adventure. We have been
permitted to explore the ultimate possibilities
of our nature, and if we might not keep this
newly-discovered territory, at least we did not
return from our travels with empty hands.
Something of the glamour lingers, something
perhaps of the wisdom, and it is with a
heightened passion, a fiercer enthusiasm, that
we set ourselves once more to our life-long
task of chalking pink salmon and pinker sun-
sets on the pavements of the world.

I once met an Englishman in the forest
that starts outside Brussels and stretches for
a long day's journey across the hills. We
found a little café under the trees, and sat in
the sun talking about modern English literature all the afternoon. In this way we discovered that we had a common standpoint
from which we judged works of art, though

our judgments differed pleasantly and provided us with materials for agreeable discussion. By the time we had divided three bottles of Gueze Lambic, the noble beer of Belgium, we had already sketched out a scheme for the ideal literary newspaper. In other words, we had achieved friendship.

When the afternoon grew suddenly cold, the Englishman led me off to tea at his house, which was half-way up the hill out of Woluwe. It was one of those modern country cottages that Belgian architects steal openly and without shame from their English confrères. We were met at the garden gate by his daughter, a dark-haired girl of fifteen or sixteen, so unreasonably beautiful that she made a disillusioned scribbler feel like a sad line out of one of the saddest poems of Francis Thompson. In my mind I christened her Monica, because I did not like her real name. The house, with its old furniture, its library, where the choice of books was clearly dictated by individual prejudices and affections, and its unambitious parade of domestic happiness, heightened my melancholy. While tea was being prepared Monica showed me the garden.

Only a few daffodils and crocuses were in bloom, but she led me to the rose garden, and told me that in the summer she could pick a great basket of roses every day. I pictured Monica to myself, gathering her roses on a breathless summer afternoon, and returned to the house feeling like a battened version of the Reverend Laurence Sterne. I knew that I had gathered all my roses, and I thought regretfully of the chill loneliness of the world that lay beyond the limits of this paradise.

This mood lingered with me during tea, and it was not till that meal was over that the miracle happened. I do not know whether it was the Englishman or his wife that wrought the magic : or perhaps it was Monica, nibbling " speculations " with her sharp white teeth ; but at all events I was led with delicate diplomacy to talk about myself, and I presently realised that I was performing the grateful labour really well. My words were warmed into life by an eloquence that is not ordinarily mine, my adjectives were neither commonplace nor far-fetched, my adverbs fell into their sockets with a sob of joy. I spoke of myself with a noble sympathy, a compassion so intense that it seemed divinely altruistic. And gradually, as the spirit of creation woke in my blood, I revealed, trembling between a natural sensitiveness and a generous abandonment of restraint, the inner life of a man of genius.

I passed lightly by his misunderstood childhood to concentrate my sympathies on the literary struggles of his youth.   I spoke of the ignoble environment, the material hardships, the masterpieces written at night to be condemned in the morning, the songs of his heart that were too great for his immature voice to sing ; and all the while I bade them watch the fire of his faith burning with a constant and quenchless flame.   I traced the development of his powers, and instanced some of his poems, my poems, which I recited so well that they sounded to me, and I swear to them also, like staves from an angelic hymn-book.   I asked their compassion for the man who, having such things in his heart, was compelled to waste his hours in sordid journalistic labours.

So by degrees I brought them to the present time, when, fatigued by a world that would not acknowledge the truth of his message, the man of genius was preparing to retire from life, in order to devote himself to the composition of five or six masterpieces. I described these masterpieces to them in outline, with a suggestive detail dashed in here and there to show how they would be finished. Nothing is easier than to describe unwritten literary masterpieces in outline ; but by that time I had thoroughly convinced my audience and myself, and we looked upon these things as completed books. The atmosphere was charged with the spirit of high endeavour, of wonderful accomplishment. I heard the Englishman breathing deeply, and through the dusk I was aware of the eyes of Monica, the wide, vague eyes of a young girl in which youth can find exactly what it pleases.

It is a good thing to be great once or twice in our lives, and that night I was wise enough to depart before the inevitable anti-climax. At the gate the Englishman pressed me warmly by the hand and begged me to honour his house with my presence again. His wife echoed the wish, and Monica looked at me with those vacant eyes, that but a few years

ago I would have charged with the wine of
my song. As I stood in the tram on my way
back to Brussels I felt like a man recovering
from a terrible debauch, and I knew that the
brief hour of my pride was over, to return,
perhaps, no more. Work was impossible to a
man who had expressed considerably more
than he had to express, so I went into a café
where there was a string band to play sentimental music over the corpse of my genius.
Chance took me to a table presided over by a
waiter I singularly detested, and the last embers
of my greatness enabled me to order my drink
in a voice so passionate that he looked at me
aghast and fled. By the time he returned
with my bock the tale was finished, and I
tried to buy his toleration with an enormous
pourboire.

No ; I will return to that house on the hill
above Woluwe no more, not even to see
Monica standing on tiptoe to pick her roses.
For I have left a giant's robe hanging on a
peg in the hall, and I would not have those
amiable people see how utterly incapable I
am of filling it under normal conditions. I
feel, besides, a kind of sentimental tenderness

for this illusion fated to have so short a life. I am no Herod to slaughter babies, and it pleases me to think that it lingers yet in that delightful house with the books and the old furniture and Monica, even though I myself shall probably never see it again, even though the Englishman watches the publishers' announcements for the masterpieces that will never appear.

A WET DAY

As we grow older it becomes more and more apparent that our moments are the ghosts of old moments, our days but pale repetitions of days that we have known in the past. It might almost be said that after a certain age we never meet a stranger or win to a new place. The palace of our soul, grown larger let us hope with the years, is haunted by little memories that creep out of corners to peep at us wistfully when we are most sure that we are alone. Sometimes we cannot hear the voice of the present for the whisperings of the past ; sometimes the room is so full of ghosts that we can hardly breathe. And yet it is often difficult to find the significance of these dead days, restored to us to disturb our sense of passing time. Why have our minds kept secret these trivial records so many years to give them to us at last when

they have no apparent consequence ? Perhaps
it is only that we are not clever enough to
read the riddle ; perhaps these trifles that we
have remembered unconsciously year after
year are in truth the tremendous forces that
have made our lives what they are.

Standing at the window this morning and
watching the rain, I suddenly became conscious of a wet morning long ago when I
stood as I stood now and saw the drops
sliding one after another down the steamy
panes. I was a boy of eight years old,
dressed in a sailor suit, and with my hair
clipped quite short like a French boy's, and
my right knee was stiff with a half-healed
cut where I had fallen on the gravel path
under the schoolroom window. It was a
really wet, grey day. I could hear the rain
dripping from the fir-trees on to the scullery
roof, and every now and then a gust of wind
drove the rain down on the soaked lawn
with a noise like breaking surf. I could hear
the water gurgling in the pipe that was
hidden by the ivy, and I saw with interest
that one of the paths was flooded, so that
a canal ran between the standard rose bushes

and recalled pictures of Venice. I thought
it would be nice if it rained truly hard and
flooded the house, so that we should all have
to starve for three weeks, and then be rescued
excitingly in boats; but I had not really any
hope. Behind me in the schoolroom my
two brothers were playing chess, but had not
yet started quarrelling, and in a corner my
little sister was patiently beating a doll.
There was a fire in the grate, but it was
one of those sombre, smoky fires in which
it is impossible to take any interest. The
clock on the mantelpiece ticked very slowly,
and I realised that an eternity of these long
seconds separated me from dinner-time. I
thought I would like to go out.

The enterprise presented certain difficulties
and dangers, but none that could not be
surpassed. I would have to steal down to
the hall and get my boots and waterproof
on unobserved. I would have to open the
front door without making too much noise,
for the other doors were well guarded by
underlings, and I would have to run down
the front drive under the eyes of many
windows. Once beyond the gate I would

be safe, for the wetness of the day would
secure me from dangerous encounters.
Walking in the rain would be pleasanter
than staying in the dull schoolroom, where
life remained unchanged for a quarter of
an hour at a time; and I remembered that
there was a little wood near our house in
which I had never been when it was raining
hard. Perhaps I would meet the magician
for whom I had looked so often in vain
on sunny days, for it was quite likely that
he preferred walking in bad weather when
no one else was about. It would be nice
to hear the drops of rain falling on the roof
of the trees, and to be quite warm and dry
underneath. Perhaps the magician would
give me a magic wand, and I would do
things like the conjurer last Christmas.

Certainly I would be punished when I
got home, for even if I were not missed
they would see that my boots were muddy
and that my waterproof was wet. I would
have no pudding for dinner and be sent to
bed in the afternoon: but these things had
happened to me before, and though I had
not liked them at the time, they did not seem

very terrible in retrospect. And life was so dull in the schoolroom that wet morning when I was eight years old!

And yet I did not go out, but stood hesitating at the window, while with every gust earth seemed to fling back its curls of rain from its shining forehead. To stand on the brink of adventure is interesting in itself, and now that I could think over the details of my expedition I was no longer bored. So I stayed dreaming till the golden moment for action was passed, and a violent exclamation from one of the chess-players called me back to a prosaic world. In a second the board was overturned and the players were locked in battle. My little sister, who had already the feminine craving for tidiness, crept out of her corner and meekly gathered the chessmen from under the feet of the combatants. I had seen it all before, and while I led my forces to the aid of the brother with whom at the moment I had some sort of alliance, I reflected that I would have done better to dare the adventure and set forth into the rainy world.

And this morning when I stood at my window, and my memory a little cruelly restored to me this vision of a day long dead, I was still of the same opinion. Oh! I should have put on my boots and my waterproof and gone down to the little wood to meet the enchanter! He would have given me the cap of invisibility, the purse of Fortunatus, and a pair of seven-league boots. He would have taught me to conquer worlds, and to leave the easy triumphs of dreamers to madmen, philosophers, and poets. He would have made me a man of action, a statesman, a soldier, a founder of cities or a digger of graves. For there are two kinds of men in the world when we have put aside the minor distinctions of shape and colour. There are the men who do things and the men who dream about them. No man can be both a dreamer and a man of action, and we are called upon to determine what rôle we shall play in life when we are too young to know what we do.

I do not believe that it was a mere wantonness of memory that preserved the image of that one hour with such affectionate detail, where so many brighter and more eventful hours have disappeared for ever. It seems to me likely enough that that moment of hesitation before the schoolroom window determined a habit of mind that has kept me dreaming ever since. For all my life I have preferred thought to action; I have never run to the little wood; I have never met the enchanter. And so this morning, when Fate played me this trick and my dream was chilled for an instant by the icy breath of the past, I did not rush out into the streets of life and lay about me with a flaming sword. No; I picked up my pen and wrote some words on a piece of paper, and lulled my shocked senses with the tranquillity of the idlest dream of all.

Milton Keynes UK
Ingram Content Group UK Ltd.
UKHW011337150124
436064UK00001B/79